The Sisterhood of Insanity

A novel by

Urban Light

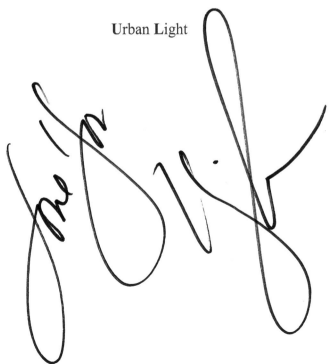

P.O. Box 1646

Austell, GA 30168

(888) 419-7009

www.urbanlightshine.com

Cover design by Artistic Revelations

Photography by Noire 3000

Edited by J. White

ISBN – 13: 978-0615416243 (URBAN LIGHT)

ISBN – 10: 0615416241

To my Lord and Savior Jesus Christ you have given me gifts to share with the world and I thank you.

ACKNOWLEDGMENTS

To my mother: you are my inspiration for wanting to succeed. You have been there for me every time I have needed you and I am so glad to share this moment with you. I can never thank you enough for giving me life.

To my son Darrell, you have sacrificed and allowed me to follow a dream. I love you so much.

To my daughter Crystal: you are my little comedian and give me laughter every day. Where would I be without the both of you in my life?

To Lila, my sister girlfriend and biggest push. You have always motivated me to shoot for the stars and not allow myself to get in the way. For all that we have been through it has paid off and I would not change one moment.

To Laurie, I would be remiss if I didn't mention you in these acknowledgments. I am so happy that the Lord has placed you in my life. You have helped me to organize and see the vision come into fruition. To my pastor, friends, church family and loved ones – always praying for me or telling me how proud you are of me, thank you for accepting all of me. I love you.

TABLE OF CONTENTS

PROLOGUE

PROLOGUE

You can find some of the most influential people in the nation living in the city of Atlanta. They shop at Phipps Plaza in Buckhead and jog at Piedmont Park in Midtown. There are civil rights leaders, Internet millionaires and huge movie producers living in some of the most prominent areas in the city and among these successful numbers are Black women.

Renee Colbert owns a three thousand square foot executive office in a high rise on Peachtree St. Every morning she stands in her corner office and looks down on the city from the twenty third floor. Her long dark brown hair pulled tightly in a bun to the back of her head while her freckles are hid by her professionally applied MAC make up done every morning by Libby who is a makeup and hair artist to the elite.

Renee feels that dressing in dark pants suits makes her look more powerful and only accents with pastels when she has to seem soft and sensitive. Most recently she wore a pink suit to a fundraiser for the cancer foundation where her company was highlighted for the huge hundred thousand dollar donation.

Numerous studies around the country have all come to the same conclusion that even though African American women are extremely successful in the work place they are more likely to be single and have a higher rate of divorce than their white counterparts. Lauren is probably one of the people in the city that Renee look down on when her only fault is loving her husband and wanting their marriage to be successful.

Older people don't believe that women were meant to endure the stressors of having to be head of household and the breadwinners. The elders may have some truth to their theory because Gena's clientele is about eighty percent women and most of them are Black women.

Lauren has heard about the famous life coach and Gena Ginger Snaps Baby and if she had access to her husband's money she would be first in the appointment book.

People pay hundreds of dollars to a Gena who is book solid for the next three months. With all the successful people going to a life coach for their emotional and sometimes spiritual advice its surprising that Pastor Brenda Miller is still in business. Although people are running to self help guru's like Gena the Pastor is not worried about her job security. Brenda spends her days and nights talking to God because when no-one else was there for her, God was. She is inspired to continue telling this message of love and acceptance from God and even if she wanted to quit Mother Hattie would never allow it.

Hattie Mae has over sixty years experience taking care of people and most people in the congregation would call her an expert while a small percentage may say that she is a busy body. Hattie's southern roots and pre civil rights upbringing have taught her love and respect that she is determined to share with others even when they don't want it or feel that they need it.

Hattie Mae is a pillar in the church community and most look to her for advice on relationships and family. She and her husband have been married for more than twenty years. Ursula would do good from Mother Hattie's advice as she is in denial over her current relationship. She never wanted to be one of those divorce statistics but she found herself divorcing her third husband and before she can even get through the pain meeting and having an affair with a much younger man.

If Gena could talk to Ursula she would probably have a lot to say but if Pastor Miller prayed about the situation it may have more impact.

While driving down Piedmont, Alana turned the radio up as loud as she could get it to drown out the loud screams from her newborn in the rear car seat. The only thing that gave her some sort of satisfaction was the motivational moment by Atlanta radio vee-jay Nikki the Diva.

Alana listens intently to the words of encouragement to all young women who had ever been in love and been hurt. She slowly drives by a homeless man on 3rd St. that reminds her of her daughter's father. It seems that almost everyone that she sees driving down the street reminds her of her lover.

Alana is going over in her mind how to make him pay for the pain that he has caused her and what consequences she may have to face. She wants to hurt him the way that he has hurt her but she doesn't want him to be so mad that he will never want to see her again. There are tons of women that seem successful on the outside and never tell anyone about their pain. These women go about their everyday lives working, playing and trying to survive never knowing how their personal hell affects us all.

The Sisterhood of Insanity

Ursula

The weatherman is telling us that we are going to be snowed in and that the roads are going to get even more slippery as the night progresses. As I look outside at the snow, it's absolutely beautiful as if God just laid a white blanket on top of every house, car and lawn in my neighborhood. It is exceptionally still for it to be 7 o'clock in the evening as if no one else is around or maybe they're all doing the same thing I'm trying to do. I look around my room and as the weatherman speaks in his monotone voice I seem to tune him out. Instead I take the time to skim over every inch of my room making sure that it is perfect.

I love my home, especially my master suite. Although my bed doesn't get put to the test, it's durable and makes a world of a difference - sleeping on a queen size pillow top. Just to lay my head on this goose down pillow makes it all feel like heaven. The gas fireplace in the corner is meticulously placed to set the ambiance. The flames make these burnt orange walls perfect for a romantic mood. My scented candles act as slaves as they burst strawberry aroma into the air with a flickering rhythmic motion. The fresh cut tulips on the dresser are just subservient enough not to over power them.

Lying on my chaise with my chenille throw across my feet is not enough for me to keep warm so I anxiously await the arrival of my human heater. I have made a list and I have checked it twice and I'm ready to be naughty because he's so damn fine. Did I put my birth control under the sink? Did I make sure I vacuumed the corners, scrubbed the toilet in my bathroom and sprayed potpourri?

I give the last scan over my bed to make sure it looks the way it looked in the Sergio Tucci magazine with the extra pillow rolls and fluffed comforter. The gold and red stripes are gorgeous and match well with these valances. Now if only I didn't have this red nail polish stain on the matching area rug everything would be perfect.

Finally the phone rings. I dang near kill myself running to it but quickly gain my composure "Hey baby are you on your way?" I try to keep from sounding too excited as if I really don't care when every inch of me is yearning for him to say he's just a corner away.

Julian is so debonair sometimes I wonder how in the hell did I snag a man that should be on the cover of a men's health magazine. My first husband was fine but didn't have a body like Julian. I mean he's 6'3 with light skin (which is usually not my cup of tea) but if you could see how fine his ass is you might change your religion; nevertheless, your preference. His hair is wavy like a deep black ocean and he wears it low as if he's in the military. He has rock hard abs, pecs and biceps of steel. I practically lose myself in his light brown eyes and forget my momma's name when he speaks to me in that deep voice. I love the fact that he's built like a wide receiver in the NFL and has the stamina to match. I don't take to much time trying to figure out why a man

this fine and 16 years my junior is with me,
instead I just enjoy every moment that we share
together and really hope that I don't do anything
to mess it up. "Naugh I ain't gonna be able to
make it tonight Ursula the weather is getting bad
and I don't want to be on the roads late when the
snow starts to freeze up."

I felt my heart shift into my throat. I
wanted to say so many things like why don't you
just bring your clothes and spend the night but I
couldn't take the answer I knew I would get. Then
I wanted to say, "its only 7:30 in the evening and
you're only 15 minutes away. I'm looking at the
same weatherman your ass is looking at and he's
saying around midnight it will start freezing."
Hell I had so many things I wanted to say but I
found myself holding my tongue about as far back
as I could without sounding so disgruntled that I'd
run him away "ok, sweetie but if you had other
plans all you had to do was tell me."

Why did I say that? Why couldn't I just
leave it at ok sweetie and tell Julian I will talk to

him some other time? I can't allow him to feel that he has me in some sort of bind or that I want him and need him as much as I do. I can't let some young ass boy feel as though he's got me whipped or that I'm some lonely ass chic sitting at home waiting on him to service her - even if that really is the case.

"Ursula I don't have any other plans. It's like I told you, I just don't want to risk my life coming all the way over there." All the way over here huh? I bet if I were a twenty-one year old with a fat ass and big tits he would risk his life, his boy's life, his daddy's and everybody else's. But I'm not! I'm a 41 year old with a big ass and little tits who goes on extreme diets trying to keep up with these young girls.

In my heart, I want to tell him so many things but I know that he just won't understand, "ok Julian" I said "ok I will just talk to you later then." I want to hurry off the telephone because I feel the tightness in my chest and the lump in my throat and there is no way I'm about to show any emotion on this call. His smooth tone came across the phone, "why you trying to rush me off the phone? I can talk for a minute." Suddenly the lump in my throat cleared and air came back in my chest as my eyes lit up and my heart stood at attention again. I will ready the treadmill and cry later, but for now I'll take his attention until he makes up some excuse to get off the phone with me, which I estimate will be around 8pm so he can get ready for the pretty young thang that he broke his date with me to see.

I am really trying to understand why in the hell I'm paying all this money every month to come in here and gasp a mouthful of musk and watch stupid Britney Spears videos on the TV. You would think that if a gym membership cost three thousand dollars a year that they would be able to afford cable or at least some decent music.

My mind is wandering off somewhere. I gotta stay focused or else I might take the risk of falling every inch of my 5'6 ass off this three foot treadmill. It's just that the very thought of him seems to constantly plague my mind. With every thought I run harder and feel as though all the blood in my body is racing towards my head. I can see the target heart rate and it's just a tad bit over my goal so I try to keep beating the hell out of this black band with my feet until these thoughts of Julian flee from my head.

After this I will work on toning my abs and probably take a quick swim before my 10am facial. I need to get it tight and keep it right, and then he will surely see what he missed out on last night. Oh here I go again drifting.

I just can't seem to understand Julian. It was only five months ago when this young portrait of perfection scooped me up. I vividly remember because it was the day when I took my Mercedes to the dealership to trade up. Julian was the finance manager and while the sales person sealed the deal with me, I could feel his eyes on me every step of the way.

I had to visit Julian briefly to make sure all of my paperwork was ready and noticed that he was extremely quiet throughout the entire process. From time to time he would ask a quick personal question here and there like "will your husband be on the loan?" or "Do you want to add any other sources of income like child support?" Just like with my second husband, I wanted Julian from the first moment I saw him. After I walked into his office I was greeted by the fresh smell of the cologne *Last Forever*. To top it off, his customer service was outstanding.

He was a little quieter than I am accustomed to because my first husband wouldn't shut up. He was always talking and trying to tell me what to do. Change can sometimes be a good thing especially when it comes packaged fine like Julian. His skin is as smooth as a baby's bottom and his lips are full, succulent and moist. After all the business in his office was done he asked me if he could call me sometime. I almost fell for the bullshit but I knew better and heard the game in every word. It's the same game my third husband ran on me when we first met and he was about 5 years younger than me. When I found out that he had four children by four *baby mamas,* the fineness wore off real quick.

A part of me loved the movement of Julian's lips knowing it was probably some rehearsed lines he used on some other older chic but he looked so good saying it. "Lie to me baby" was what my mind said but my heart knew better. I heard myself say "Now Ursula, you are a smart, educated and highly sophisticated woman and men are dogs so don't fall in love - fall into train mode". I think I could be a fabulous teacher for this cute lil puppy that I'm trying to decide if I'm going to take home.

My heart was telling me to leave him alone and my spirit was saying run but I did neither. Instead, I analyzed the situation and allowed my mind to tell me that somehow this young man will be so enthralled with me that my every word will thrill him and keep him engaged

17

on me. I felt that somehow his age would dictate how this relationship would go and that it would only be in my favor. After all, I had been around the block and through the woods with three marriages under my belt. I know a thing or two about men. Besides, I'm not gonna let some 25 year old play me or run no game that I haven't seen. Or has he already?

Finally the timer goes off on the treadmill waking me from my Julian stupor. Time for a quick shower and off to work I go.

"Good morning Ms. Woods, I just received a call from the Grace International Missionary Church that they are ready to approve the design of Pastor Miller's office." Ms. Ella is an amazing assistant. I just wish she wouldn't call me when she knows I'm just leaving the gym.

"Ok Ms. Ella please place them on the schedule for next week. I have Colbert and Associates to finish this week and I'm waiting for the new fabric".

I feel so rushed because this lady Ms. Colbert puts the capital B in the word for female dog. And although I can't stand her, I refuse to call another black woman that word even though so many black men seem to love to have it rolling off of their tongues like they're getting paid to say it. The funny thing is most of them are getting paid to degrade us. Besides her staff always has my check ready and waiting.

I have been working for Colbert and Associates for about 3 years since Ms. Colbert branched off from Hughes, Sacks and Jasowski. She has been in almost every business magazine there is when it comes to the fabulous and under forty. She is the "it girl" of Atlanta and is one of this cities elite. I just wish the heifer had a heart because if I did have a husband or family, my staff and I would never get a chance to see them. When you start a project with her you must be perfect and you must finish on the date and deadline you provided because this woman possesses the power to literally destroy you and trust me, I've seen and heard about many of her casualties.

"Good morning Heraldo, has your team completed the lighting for the conference room?" Heraldo is my go to guy for lighting and any thing electrical. He has worked with me for the past 20 years and there is no one more reliable or dependable. It's ironic that my second husband Steven introduced me to Heraldo when the main reason that he divorced me is because he said I criticized and accused him of not being reliable or dependable.

"Yes Ursula the team has completed the job and I think that you'll be pleased. I am happy to advise you that we are on schedule and will be out of here today!"

"Great job Heraldo that's like music to my ears!" That means that now that the job is complete, my check will be in the mail and I can set up my appointment for my breast implants.

Coming up on the elevator to this office is always bittersweet since I was the one who recommended my second husband to do the work - the now highly respected architect Christopher Simms. He was a hard sell because even though her team won't admit it, I think Ms. Colbert has an issue working with black people and especially black women.

Her office contracted Mich'ele Designs and when we started our first project, my partner Michelle O'Rory met with her. They had a fabulous meeting but when I arrived to do the work it seemed that she was disappointed that I was a black woman. Now all these years later we have done exceptional work for her but she still never meets with me but instead defers to Michelle for any questions as if I could not give them to her. It's quite alright. I am used to rejection because in business just like everything else, rejection is the fuel to the fire of success. I proved to her that not only could I do the work but also gave her so many incentives that as a

21

Business Person she could do nothing but acknowledge our perfection.

Looking at the beautiful clear glass elevator with mahogany wood trim I think that Ms. Colbert, as hard of a sale as she was, even had to buy the beauty of Chris Simms though I couldn't.

It's 2am and I can't sleep. My hands feel numb so I start doing jump n jacks, running in place and push-ups. Although my body is tired, I couldn't sleep longer than 15 minutes. I can't get any peace knowing what I just did. It's my birthday weekend and to treat myself I got a suite at my own expense at one of the most expensive hotels in Atlanta. I wanted to be served with room service, bell service, valet and a coochie tune up. It was not my intention to be screwed by Julian but somehow I managed to allow this to happen again. Now I feel empty. I keep standing in the middle of the room thinking about what transpired earlier. How could I have done things differently? So I retrace my steps from the beginning from when he first came to the room.

"What's up Ursula? Why are you rushing?" I wanted to be ready so that when he finally came over to my hotel room we could go out to a club and dance some before coming back to the room and ending the evening with candles, champagne and some serious love making.

"I am trying to get ready so that we can at least catch a club or something."

Julian sits his ass on the couch and lays back and just looks at me as if I'm crazy.

"You wanted to go out? It's late and I have to go to work in the morning, plus you didn't say anything about wanting to go out."

I don't want to argue with him which I feel is exactly what he wants me to do so he will have some excuse to leave. So instead I crawled on top of his lap wearing only my bra and panties.

"I bought something for you baby."

Julian looked surprised as I let the air out of the balloon he was trying to explode to get out of this evening.

"Wow Ursula, you bought me something on your birthday? How sweet."

I was furious that it took him hours to come over and about the fact that I really wanted to go out but I was going to maintain control of this situation because it is my birthday.

"Yes Your Fineness! I saw these cuff links while I was out shopping for my new dress and thought that they would fit you perfectly."

We still didn't go out but he smiled at me, ensured that he had love for me, then took off the remainder of my clothes.

Maybe if he wouldn't have left so soon after his last nut I wouldn't feel so bad. Even after I shared in conversation with him that I really wanted this to be special and asked him to spend the night with me, he left.

"I have to go to work tomorrow Ursula."

Now I'm laying in my beautiful four hundred dollar a night boudoir feeling like a five-dollar ho. I knew when my lonely ass called him at nine o'clock at night and he said he was putting his clothes back on after being off three hours what his intentions were but I still let him come over. I knew when he didn't get to the room until eleven and asked me not to dress up to go out after I got out the shower what his intentions were, but I still let him kiss and caress me. I knew when he took off his clothes and asked me to get on my knees, which happens to be his preferred position, that he didn't have an emotional connection to me but I still let him inside me.

He never told me he loved me. He never said that he wanted to spend the night. He never even said that he was my boyfriend but over and over again I still give him the best of me. The very part of me that I'd been saving for that special person and this special occasion! What the hell is wrong with me?

Renee
Colbert

Click! That is the only response that this
woman is going to get from me. I am not even
going to give her the pleasure of hearing a reply to
her nonsense.

Kelly and I have been friends since
childhood but just like everyone else from my old
life, I will delete her. I will no longer make
excuses for my success just because they can't
understand it.

Ignorant people with no education are
appalling to me but Kelly went to Midlothian
College the same as I did and worked her way
through the same way that I did. The only
disappointment to me with Kelly is that she
decided to graduate college, get married, have
children and stay at home. What a waste of a
good education and what a waste of life. To think
that I even take my precious time talking with her
is sometimes mind boggling to me. She found
Jesus and now wants to always tell me about what
Jesus has done in her life and how he can change

27

my life and how he loves me. Her husband is suppose to be something in the church and they still live in my small town of Brilliant, Alabama which has a population of about eight hundred people and fifteen of those are my brothers and sisters. Kelly talks about how wonderful the Lord is and how much he does for her yet she is still in the same place wasting her life doing absolutely nothing,

Meanwhile, I am the youngest of the fifteen and amazingly the only one who got out and made something of myself. If you sneeze you will miss the town on the map but when it comes to poverty they take the cake. This is why there is no need for me to ever go back there or to deal with the leeches called family who never call you except to ask for money. I tell Kelly not to ever give them my number but for some reason I've had to change my number three times over the past year. This is the final straw for her if she wants to continue to have the honor of speaking with me. She must not allow my number to "slip" out again.

Kelly called me to wish me a happy birthday of which she could have simply sent me a text or an email. Instead, to lure me into her foolishness she decided to call me.

"Renee, are you going to at least call the young man that I tried to hook you up with? I know he isn't rich but he is a wonderful man and I really want you to be happy on your birthday."

I am so tired of Kelly thinking that I must have a man in order to be happy or that somehow a man will sweep me off my feet. I am to busy for a relationship and what do I need with a man?

"I am more than happy! I drive a Mercedes SLR McLaren and have a brand-new Phantom with driver included. I live in a 2.5 million-dollar mansion and have a vacation home in Miami. Happy is having money and I have more than most men can even think of having - especially black men!"

The truth of the matter is that I am tired of feeling like I'm in competition with some man because of his inferiority complex. Most men especially black men are insecure and will never reach my level. I am tired of hearing that men are intimidated by me and my success and tired of them trying to come into my life to control me. I will not dumb down for them and I will not lower my standards!

The problem with most women especially black women is that they just accept anything because they want a man but I believe that a woman should have her own and a real man will be able to handle a strong black woman.

"I hear you talking about material things Ne-Ne but what about love? This guy Donald is really a good man."

I have already told Kelly several times that if the man is not at least six feet four inches and has a six figure income or greater that there is no need to even try to introduce me.

"Please Kelly don't start with this. I am appreciative of the birthday wishes and please tell your parents thank you for the birthday card but I really must get back to work."

And just as the days are long she started in on me with her mess.

"Renee all you do is work, when are you going to take some time and smell the roses? I mean you are never going to find a man if you are always working. When you take trips you always take them alone and you know it's not good for a woman to be alone or else God wouldn't have made man. You are too pretty to be a lesbian and I know a lot of that is going on now in these big cities. I mean if you are its quite alright, I'm just saying it would be a sin and you would probably go to hell but I will still accept you. Oh my God and if you wait any longer to have children your going to be to old to run behind them and..."

She just goes on and on about the bible and why I need to be married which is the main reason why I have placed her number in the do not answer log. Most of the time I answer just in case something happens to my parents. This way she can always reach me to let me know. Then she takes it to the ultimate extreme and I have to finally hang up the telephone.

"Renee how can you call yourself successful when you have no husband, no kids and nothing substantial in your life? Would you like to accept Jesus into your heart?"

Click!

"Ms. Colbert is there anything else that you need for me to do?"

Cicley humbly asks as she is closing out for the day.

"Cicley, did you make sure that Mr. Peterson has my final report and are the designers finished with the conference room?"

I don't and will not accept anything less than the best. So far Cicley has worked out well as she was educated at Harvard graduate school like me and trained by me. The last three executive assistants that I had could not cut the mustard and I am sorry if having a personal life is more important to them than being successful.

My last assistant Lauren only lasted a few hours. She was sent to me highly recommended by this staffing agency that I later found out was business partners with her husband. I don't have time to take housewives and make them into professionals. Either you are committed to my success which will ultimately lead to your success or you take your ass home.

"Yes Ma am, I made sure that he had an email copy and a hard copy for tomorrows conference in our newly decorated and completed conference room." All I could think to myself is that this young lady is well on her way. "Very well then I will see you at 6am." The lights go out in her office "I will keep my blackberry by my side Ms. Colbert per your instructions and make sure that I pick up your latte or did you want an espresso?" Well done is all that I can think. " A latte will be fine. Have a good evening."

What most people such as Kelly don't understand is that hard work and dedication will always lead to success. Her question to me is so damn ridiculous that she deserves to be hung up on and I will make no apologies for it.

"How can I call myself successful when I have no kids, never been married and have nothing substantial?"

I can't believe she could ask me that question. I run a multi-million dollar company, make three hundred twenty five thousand dollars per year as a consultant with Silverman and Scwab, and was the first and only African American female to hold the position of Vice President of Marketing at Hughes, Sacks and Jasowski before launching the legacy that I call my firm. Because of my success, I've been featured in magazines, newspapers, television and radio. My home is probably six thousand square feet more than her home and that's only the home in Atlanta. My home in Florida is smaller but hell, at least I have two.

Kelly is the one who called me when her husband was laid off and she needed money for bills. If marriage was so beautiful and her husband is such a wonderful man then why the hell couldn't she tell him that she got the money from me instead of making up some lie that she won the lottery? It's amazing to me how happy she claims to be when she is constantly complaining about the raggedy car that she drives and how she wants him to buy her a new one but they can't afford it right now. Then to think that I invited them to my spring mixer at my home and they come damn near dressed alike with pastels of all colors.

Besides, marriage is for women who need a man to take care of them. So as long as God allows me to take care of myself then I will do it. The only reason I would get married is if the right man comes along and is more successful than I am and is ready to take me to the next level in my life. I would only consider a man that is more powerful, more educated and more driven than I.

The past relationships that I have had have only left me holding the bag because some man couldn't handle the fact that I was more successful or made more money than he did. They said that I was demeaning and demanding when again it's their own insecurities. Why am I sitting here even thinking about this conversation when I just looked at the hundred-dollar bill in my purse that says *In God We Trust*? So yes Kelly, I have plenty of God in my life!

"Murray, have the car waiting at the front door, I will be leaving the office in about ten minutes."

My career has always been there for me and is one of my greatest investments. I put hard work and dedication into it and I get back a huge return on my investment. I think that I have mastered the men department because I think of them as a commodity and not a necessity. I will never be the one who stoops so low as to ask some man out. And paying is definitely out of the question!

About a month ago I met Mr. Commodity while I was practicing my swing at this exclusive golf club in Flowery Branch. My Soror wanted me to come to the club and meet her on the driving range hoping that if I came out she would actually get the motivation to see it through. I went to the club reluctantly but to my surprise there was this astute young judge name Reginald Van Horn that happened to catch my eye.

At the time the white girls were all over him because not only is he exceptionally good looking, but he only comes to the club on Thursday and Saturday. Every other guy seemed to be regulars so he was the safe nobody knew how to crack. Fresh fish! I knew when I saw him that I wouldn't have to do much for him to pay attention and since "marketing" is what I do, I made myself the best advertisement.

I learned from white women about which men are worth my time and how to catch their attention. Reginald, being a black man was not necessarily my type but his family's last name and impeccable reputation along with their old money were more than appealing. I knew exactly what my plan of action would be to snag this man.

The next time I went to the club as a guest to Marcie on a Saturday because I now knew Reginald's schedule. I made sure that Marcie, her husband and I took time out to have some fun. I would have my wonderful Soror tell her husband that I was thinking about joining and like a basketball team that sends out their star player; they recruited Reginald to convince me. He is successful, single and has a lot of influence. Not to my surprise, there is much talk about him being elected to the state supreme court.

It's a new year and to celebrate exceeding my goals, I decided to give Reginald an opportunity to impress me. He will really have to use his imagination because I have had others that have tried and failed.

I really think Reginald can accomplish the task. I see his competitive edge. I have played tennis with him a few times at the club so when he asked me out I was not surprised.

Thus far we have amazing intellectual conversation while we dine at the most prominent restaurant with delegates and other socialites. Kelly would never be able to dine in a spot like this.

I will not make a mistake so therefore my plan with this man must be flawless. Kelly says that I act and think like a man because I'm not lovey-dovey and touchy-feely with these men.

I am numb to the point that I don't feel anything anymore. During my college years I tried love and tried to follow the mantra that my mother taught me.

"Find a good man, love him and he will take care of you."

After about the third man cheating on me I learned that I needed to approach men like my stocks. If they make you money fine, but as soon as you see that they are less than they're worth, dump'em.

I think this lesson came to fruition during my senior year in college with a man that Kelly introduced me to by the name of Peter Myles. From what I remember from my days of being a weak woman, Peter is the one that had me questioning myself. I thought everything with him was great until I saw him with Heather Walker. I found myself hurt and in tears constantly asking "What is wrong with me?"

My analytical mind told me that I was the common denominator. Therefore I changed my way of thinking and instead of the so-called unattainable love my mother said I should look for, I looked for success. Now, the only other thing that I wish I could change is my complexion. I am already very fair but I know that the brighter I am, the better.

Everything else about me is perfect. I am rich, independent with no kids, never been married, graduate of a well respected university and not to mention beautiful. My 5'8 size four frame, coupled with a six-figure income should have Reginald smitten. If that doesn't work then I'll pull more punches by letting down my eighteen inches of Remy hair flown in direct from Indonesia and show these white girls what real money can buy.

Reginald comes after a long dormant phase of nothing but celibacy and self-reflection. My life coach Gena told me that I needed to take some time to think about why I'm so dependent on me. She's a jazz artist, life coach and best selling author. She came highly recommended. Most of the rich and famous hire her so when it came to my life plan, she was a no-brainer. I also took time to get connected with my softer side since my mother constantly says that I am to cold. Kelly says the same thing and since I have an increase of women client's I figured being more sensitive will help me seal the deal.

During the beginning phase of my sessions with Gena I gave up men and sex and put myself in utter seclusion. I didn't even look at men during this phase. Thank God that this phase is over because I may have missed out on Reginald.

I hate going to church. I don't know why I ever agreed to do this. I knew these black women would be jealous of me. Seems that if you are half decent looking and a new face at a church every woman who is married thinks you are there to take her husband, even if the church does have ten thousand members. The only reason I agreed to come to this funeral is because I know that dignitaries, politicians and probably every news media in the state will be here. I am among the elite so of course I'll have front row seats with Reginald. His family was close to the 'civil rights' leaders.

My driver had already dropped me at the destination where I saw Reginald, his brother Senator Brian Van Horn and their parents come in. I soon learned from my assistant that Reginald is a trustee of Grace International Non-Denominational Church and although he has invited me before, his pastor is a woman and I don't believe in women being pastors. I made an exception because this is a funeral and a world famous televangelist Bishop was the speaker for the eulogy.

"Hello Renee, I'm really glad you decided to attend service."

The one reason that I came is to have an opportunity to have Reginald introduce me to his parents. Once he does that, I know it's only a matter of time before we seal the deal. Plus I want the front row seats to the media because the exposure would show those women client's that I have some compassion.

Placing a somber smile on my face I cordially responded, "Judge Van Horn it's good to see you as well."

He shook my hand, slowly walked over to his parents and they took their seats. I am in utter disbelief! Where are my front row seats and why didn't he introduce me to his parents? Doesn't this nigga know who I am!

Reverend Brenda Miller

Today I woke up and just laid in the bed. I know that it's Sunday and that I am supposed to go to church and be a good little Christian but I really don't feel like it. I just want to lay in my bed, watch some TV and not deal with people today.

"All these years that I've been with you. All this time and you still have me suffering? I thought that you said you would give me the desires of my heart?"

Sometimes I just feel so lonely even when I'm in a crowded church full of people that tell me that they love me. Why am I constantly holding on to my celibate state when I really want to be held by a man and have him tell me that he loves me? Now don't get me wrong, Jesus is enough for me or at least He was.

"Lord, I don't want to seem ungrateful because I'm really not but today I'm lonely."

Where is my faith! I need to stop this but I am just tired of disappointment. I mean at first I thought that maybe I was single because I was not ready for a husband so therefore I took years working on being whole spiritually and growing in God. Then when my emotions started to get the best of me I would see a therapist and work on my emotions.

"I remember you being there for me, especially through those emotional moments. I haven't forgotten."

My weight seems to be that whole "thorn in the flesh" thing that gets me. I love food and with church being my life, food seems to be in a never-ending supply. Seems that everything that we do as church folk has food included in it. Last Sunday was the church anniversary and after service the ladies cooked up fried chicken, baked chicken, string beans, mashed potatoes and rolls. Then there were the pies, cakes and an endless supply of sweet tea.

"You're really gonna have to help me with this devil called my weight that seems to go up and down like a yo-yo. Maybe if you don't hear mc on the husband thing, since this is my temple and you told us to take care of our temples, maybe you'll help me. I am so tired."

At the beginning of last year one of my members started the *Faithful Few Boot Camp* and encouraged me to join. As a servant leader I'm compelled to support, especially when my support would be a huge benefit to my body.

I figured that it couldn't hurt because even though I am a beautiful woman, most men are attracted to the physical first. After they see what they like then they want to get to know you better. Junk in the trunk is fine but I had a whole bus that I needed to park. This being the case, I took all of last year and worked out early in the morning and late at night.

"We did pretty good didn't we Lord. So how did I gain twelve pounds?"

Years ago I placed myself in a position were sex wouldn't be able to creep into my relationship because sex causes an emotional tie and the inability to see the person for who they really are. So for eighteen years I stopped dating and made sanctification my goal.

"I've been totally committed to you for over eighteen years and this is what I get!"

I think that through the years I have done well as far as my emotions are concerned. I needed to get rid of the baggage from a divorce at the age of twenty and from other past relationships.

"I remember feeling your spirit and you leading me to call all the people that had hurt me and forgive them."

It was extremely hard to forgive my ex-husband and put away the past but with the Holy Spirit I did it and forgiveness is so freeing.

"I should have done it a long time ago."

The spiritual part of my journey came after I finally accepted my call into ministry and began to move in the power of God.

"Looking back 20 years when you and I first started this whole process, I never would have thought that you would use me the way that you have."

A congregation of six thousand, television ministry, homeless shelters, recovery homes and constant financial blessings! I have preached until I have almost passed out, visited more sick people than Ghandi and led so many to Christ that I feel like the female Billy Graham.

"With all that I have done for you and all that you have done for me I just don't understand why it is that the one thing I desire the most you still won't give me!"

"Pastor, we have everything ready for the Bishop's arrival do you need someone to come and pick you up?"

Ms. Hattie calls me on the phone every Sunday morning and gives me a first hand report of what the *women's committee* has done. She provides leadership to the women's committee, the lay organization, the greeters and gives input in almost every other committee in the church. I

am glad that even though I seem to be in my
stupor, God always has a way of giving me a
reason to get up in the morning. I almost forgot
that Bishop Jones was coming to our church to
preach but I can always depend on Sister Hattie.
She is truly someone that takes care of the
necessities and gets the task accomplished. She
takes good care of the church and I. Just make
sure that you are never one to get on her bad side
or there is a whole different person that you may
have to bind.

"Good morning Sister Hattie thanks for
calling me and thank you and your committee for
taking care of everything with the Bishop. I am
going to drive myself to church and will get there
about an hour before service to speak with Bishop
and his wife."

"Ok Pastor, we will make sure that we
make them comfortable until you arrive and if you
need anything at all just let me know and I'll
make sure that Sista Evans and the ladies get it
done."

"Ok Lord I got your message. You just can't seem to leave me alone huh?"

I finally get up and slowly walk my large body over to the shower and slowly turn on the water. Its hard for me to get dressed but not because I can't find anything to wear. In my walk in closet there's an array of suits still in the plastic from the cleaners.

I don't usually put on make-up but there are going to be so many people in the church today that I don't want to look too much like a plain Jane. Plus I have to take pictures with Bishop Jones and his wife. I don't feel like doing this. I need some extra strength. Unable to withstand anymore overload of thoughts and pressures from the schedule of the day, I finally submit and fall on my knees.

"Dear Lord, please help me to get through this day. I know it seems that I am whining and that I am not grateful but I am. I need you to be with me. Please don't take your Spirit from me. I need you and although I don't have a husband I

52

am wise enough to know that you are my
covering. Please order my steps and bless all of
the events that will happen today. Please
strengthen me and protect my mind from evil.
Help me please. It's me Brenda your servant.
Please help me to get through the day and just
simply place one foot in front of the other. I can't
do this without you. Amen."

My secretary sent my schedule earlier in the week and after the Bishop leaves us, we have two funerals and one wedding. This doesn't make this the most encouraging week. It seems that more people are dying than people getting married and for the ones that are getting married they seem to get divorced. There are more babies being born out of marriage meaning that there are more single parents. There are more people in the church getting divorced than people who aren't Christians. Thank God the people I marry aren't getting divorced or else I would probably just quit cause I am already worn out.

"When is my sabbatical?"

I think I am going to take one this year and go to Egypt or Ireland. I am just tired of being around big cities where the people have so many problems and think somehow that I am Jesus and can save them from them all.

Right now driving in this car down the street and seeing all the homeless people and all the hopelessness saddens my heart. We gave over five hundred families clothes last month and assistance but it just seems that we are not making a dent. Our clothing stores and food kitchens around the city are almost depleted from helping those that are hungry and out of work. I am trying to stop crying right now.

"Lord, where are you and why are you allowing your people to suffer? I am trying trying trying so hard please just let me know what I'm doing wrong!   What more do you want me to do? I just can't take seeing this hurt on your people".

It's hard to drive and cry uncontrollably but somehow I make it into the parking lot. I have to stop and look in the mirror to make sure that my eyes are wiped because I can't let one of my members see me having a breakdown in my car. Seems that as soon as I wipe my tears here comes another one running down my face.

"Lord, help me! I just want to be right so please stop these tears and move my legs so that I can get out of this car and get in this church."

"God morning Bishop it's so good to see you. I trust you had a wonderful flight."
He stands and has a bold stature that is almost like an angel standing in my presence.

"Pastor Miller every time I come to your church I am always greeted with excellence. I love the new entry of the church it is glorious."

I watch as he pulls his wife near so that she can put her two cents in and not feel left out.

"Yes Pastor. The Bishop and I were admiring the new entrance and decorations. They are wonderful.   You must give us the information of the company that did your work."

I love preacher's wives they are always so careful of what they say as if they have rehearsed all of their lives. I have found that they can be some of the most powerful women that you ever want to meet, schooling you on how to get your foot into this boys club called ministry and still maintaining their sweet persona. First Lady Jones was one of my strongest allies in getting appointed to this church and I have paid her back by making sure that her sister Hattie maintains some of the most prominent positions and gets accolades and recognition for almost everything.

"I will make sure to get you all the information for Mich'ele Designs, now let's go ahead and get ready for service as I heard it is standing room only."

The Bishop is a prominent figure and some people follow him from state to state so I knew that today was going to be dynamic and powerful. God knows just what I need when I need it.

I just woke up and I missed church. Thank God it's fourth Sunday and my youth pastor will be preaching. I think one part of me wanted too.

"What is happening to us Lord? My spirit longs to have that awesome relationship I had with you before my father died."

I can't seem to stop crying.

"Why God why am I alone? What did I do to make you want to punish me? Just tell me what I have done and I will try to make it better!"

I feel so double minded. It's like on one hand God has done so much for me materially and spiritually but on the other he is punishing me for something but for whatever reason he is not revealing it to me. I just can't understand what more I am supposed to do.

"Wait on the Lord again I say wait. That's what I preach when I go to singles conferences and tell others but Lord how long are we supposed to wait?"

I preach, teach and do all that I feel that God wants me to do and still have to come home to an empty house.

"Lord, I don't understand why I have sacrificed now for 18 years and as much as I love intimacy why you won't allow me to have it. Didn't you say that it is not good to burn?"

Why am I trying to reason with God when I know that He does what He wants to do when He wants to do it?

"I didn't sign up for this. I was not meant to be a nun, not getting none, not doing none and not having none."

I need to take a shower and then maybe I will feel better.

"Lord I can't take it anymore. It's not about sex okay its just not! It's about companionship. I don't have any prospects for marriage, no black books, or anything!"

I don't want to face the consequences or risk going out in the street and just giving it away to some brother. Surely that would be ridiculous. It would be just my luck that I would end up on some gossip show. I can see it now. The headlines would read, '*Television Preacher Sex Scandal.*' It's so hard. It seems like I go through this almost every Valentines Day and I am tired of faking the funk - spending all that money on flowers to send to myself.

I preach at women conferences about being lonely and they are set free but I continue to suffer from loneliness. I have had the wonderful privilege of being an author of several relationship books for singles but I wonder why my advice seems to work for everyone else except for me. In my bestseller '*Marry Jesus*' I tell them to hold on and be strong and have had letters from women who swear that the Lord brought them their husband as soon as they closed the last chapter. Yet I'm the one that wrote the book with the inspiration of the Lord of course and have yet to find My Jesus in the flesh.

"I just don't know how much more of this I can take!"

I am so ready for my trip.

"Thank you Lord." This is the last day of the longest minister's conference I think I've ever been a part of. I won't complain though because I did get a spiritual revival. I was just leaving the final session, networking with the last Pastor when I was stopped in my tracks by a lean, tall, dark skin man. Only God could produce such a work because this man was blessed from the top of his clean-cut head to the soles of what had to be size sixteen feet. I had to ask about him through my friend the Reverend Dr. Geneva Richey, who knows everything and everyone at the conference.

"I think he's single Brenda. You know what, he is single. As a matter fact, he's the Assistant Pastor of New Mount Olive Baptist Church in Detroit."

Hmmm a well established church in Detroit and he's single! I was surprised to find out that he is single but when I found out I had to ask God.

"Ok Lord I'll approach if I know that you are with me but I'm not going to keep doing this and getting disappointed. If this is not the one I'm telling you I quit! I can't keep doing this so there you go. I love you first and no man can ever take your place. You know that so please tell me something! Show me something."

Right when I was about to smoothly sashay this beautiful five seven big hip physique over to him and introduce myself, here comes Bishop Jones. I almost cursed. What in the hell does he want? We've been in each other's face for the past five days of this conference.

"Brenda how you doing? You and Geneva always bring a lot of light when you ladies walk in the room."

Please go away was what I wanted to say but he's my spiritual daddy so okay here it goes.

Smile Brenda play the game - Let the Lord use ya as they say.

"All is well Bishop. This has been a wonderful conference and I have enjoyed every moment - especially your sermon on spiritual warfare."

Geneva was very hip to the game as well. Her and her husband were both ordained by the Bishop so we both smiled and closed our mouths to wait on our daddy to give us another personal sermon.

"Amen Amen I am so glad that the Lord spoke. Come here, there's someone I'd like you all to meet."

Lord could it really be that the Bishop himself was going to make the introduction of Angel man and me. Surely if there were ever an undeniable answer from God this one had to be it. We walked over with the Bishop and he did his introductions and told us how this young handsome preacher man was changing the face of the city.

I had looked at him for the last hour but I made sure not to stay around him too long. I just wanted to give him a whiff of my perfume and a close look at my flawless mocha skin. It worked because as soon as I was headed out the door, the Rev. Marquis Mitchell came running behind me. "Do you want me to walk you to your car?" It's summer in the inner city, the church has security all over and I know that Jesus walks with me but it was great to have a man finally ask me. I wish I had time to have a deep conversation or coffee but an exchange of numbers will do. For now, it's off to the airport and back to my lonely home.

It's a beautiful night. God is the master artist. I see his glory in everything. "Lord you are so awesome." The sun is going down and finally I have some free time. I think its time to finally find out what Rev. Marquis is all about "Hello may I speak to Marquis?" With a deep voice I hear his sultry, soothing and kind hello come over the phone.

" Hello Brenda! How are you today?"

We go through the same old motions of fine and fine. We ask about kids but neither of us have any of our own. We ask about music, movies and make simple conversation then all of a sudden he plays some old grooves through the telephone "I want a groove with you" sung as only the Isleys can sing it.

Finally, someone who understands that preachers are people too and that just because we listen to R&B, we are not bound for hell. This man understands the trials that I go through. I feel like I can be Brenda whenever I'm with him and not Reverend Miller. Sometimes church folks don't understand that we are not supernatural or superhuman but that we have emotions and feel anger too. With every word that he spoke I felt like I was in heaven and truly enjoyed our conversation from nine at night until two o'clock in the morning.

"Good night Brenda! Sweet dreams."

Sweet dreams were in my mind and for the first time in a long time butterflies were in my stomach.

"Good night Marquis! I will talk to you later."

Alana

"I am beginning to wonder if I am some sort of masochist. Do I subconsciously love or like for you to hurt me?"

When it comes to men in my life that I have loved, they have been dysfunctional. First, it was Raymar and now Craig. All of them end up hurting me. I don't understand why I keep doing the same thing and expect a different result. I believe somebody told me that this is insanity.

"I do love you, but sometimes I wonder why is it that I love you more than I love myself? I say this because if I loved myself more than I loved you or even had the least bit of self esteem, I wouldn't continue to allow you to treat me like this."

Click! Oh my God, I know he didn't just hang up on me.

Although I know it's wrong, I continue to allow myself to be subjected to his treatment. Like I'm his plaything. Of course Craig says that he doesn't use me and then he reminds me how he has paid for my car, taken me on trips, bought me jewelry and all of the wall banging sex that we've had.

When it all comes down to it, I didn't want, ask or really need any of those things from him. I asked for commitment for over the past three years and he has yet to give it to me. Every time I ask, there's always another excuse or gift to pacify me into getting off the subject. Now after all this time has passed, to add insult to injury, I allowed myself to slip up and get pregnant.

"I wonder if he'll treat our daughter the way he's treated me and give her some lame ass excuses and pipe dreams of spending time with her or is he going to hide her from the world and his wife and pretend that she does not exist?"

I am not going to allow Craig to get off that easy. This is why phones are made with automatic redial.

"Hello, why do you keep calling me like this Alana?"

" I just want to finish. Yes you have done ok so far but our baby is only a month old. Yes you have bought a couple of packs of diapers, car seat, wet wipes and an Easter outfit but lets see how long it's going to last. I mean I really want it to last for the next 18 years even if you and I are not together."

I sugar coated the last part of the conversation when I really wanted to say

"You scare me sometimes because you are nice and cuddly one day and then tell me we don't have a relationship the next and threaten me with your legal jargon."

I don't know what to believe and now three years and two suicide attempts later I still don't have a man that I can call all mine. Yeah; looking back three years seems like a lifetime. I have put so much love and energy into this but I know that I need to let you go.

Like the old saying goes *"if you love somebody let them go and if they come back to you they were really yours but if they don't they never was."*

     I don't really know if this is true or not but this is a whole new year and Craig and I are about to sit down next week for a heart to heart talk. Although I don't feel like he feels what I'm saying, one thing I do know is that he's gonna listen to me. If nothing else, maybe I just need to take these three days without him to figure out what I really want to do. I need to write my thoughts on a sheet of paper then sit down and talk to him. That way I am not getting off track and letting the emotions get in the way and sounding like I'm rambling.

     My rambling is aggravating to both of us because he really tunes me out and I need him to listen. So I will take the time to write the five important points on paper of exactly what I want to talk about and what I need answers to.

     This whole day has been crazy. The baby has constantly been crying and I need to finish this last paper for school so that I can turn it in to Professor Robinson who says that I have a great chance of being Magna Cum Laude.

But before I finish all of that I have to call Craig. I have called him twice today and sent him a text but he still hasn't returned my messages. He came over last night and we made love for the first time in a long time and afterward he held me very tight. I woke up this morning and he was gone. He didn't even wake me up to tell me he was leaving. When I went to take the baby to the sitter I didn't have any gas in my car. Whether he wants to hear it or not, I am not going to hold it in. I'm calling him right now.

"Hello Mr. Heart.....breaker! You are like an addiction to me! I want to let you go but it is so hard. I guess deep down I know the truth, which is no matter how many babies I have or how much I tell you that I love you, you are not leaving your wife. I am not going to live happily ever after with you am I?"

That fantasy is the reason why I've held on this long thinking that love will conquer all and that he feels the deep passionate Love for me that I feel for him.

"Alana, why are you doing this to yourself and why are you doing this to us?"

Craig's voice is so commanding that it makes me shut up. Plus, authority in my life is what I feel I need. Sure we've had our arguments - what couples don't? When it's really love you don't sweat the small stuff and somehow you get through it. Then again that's my problem, thinking that somehow he felt the same. I mean, why would he? If a man can have a beautiful, younger woman on the side that does everything that his wife won't do and still be able to have the stability and luxuries of having a wife, why would he leave?

It is so pathetic when I think about it. I am a twenty-three year old woman about to graduate from college having wasted my time and my life with a man who will never be mine. I have gone through every emotion in the spectrum: love, hate and anger. I have loved him deeper than any man I've ever known including my abusive father. And it still isn't enough for him.

"I hate you because you led me to believe that you would leave your wife for me when I had the first abortion. Ok, you never said 'I am leaving my wife for you, but you did tell me to have the abortion so it can be just us. Then to turn around and tell me never to leave you and give me examples of your friends that have left their wives for their mistresses."

Craig buts in, "Alana, stop this crying and complaining and torturing of yourself and me! It just sounds to me like my love is not enough for you and that you need somebody that will love you the way you need to be loved."

What have I done? Craig sounds like he is trying to break up with me. I don't want him to leave me and I don't want to live without seeing him. I need to change my tone quick before he hangs up again - this time for the last time. He alrcady told mc that if I take him to court for child support he'll never come and see his daughter and will cut me off completely. By him being a lawyer, I don't want to risk being railroaded by some of his judge and lawyer cronies if I go to court.

"I'm sorry. I'm just a little upset because you are going away for three days and I can't go with you. I also had a really rough morning and have a lot of school work to do."

I try really hard to sweeten up my tone because he is the type that once he is done with you, he is really done with you.

"It's just that you used to do everything with me and I miss doing things with you."

I am waiting to hear the tone he is going to use with me now that I have at least apologized.

"I told you that if you had the baby it was not going to be the same and what do you do - hide it from me until your eighth month and now you want me to be forthcoming. You should really be thankful Alana that I am even still with you after a stunt like that."

I hear him but it doesn't seem to matter what he says because I can't stop crying. Maybe it's totally my fault for feeling this way - expecting too much, wanting him like I do. Who knows, maybe if I had him all to myself I wouldn't want him anymore. Or I might be miserable thinking that he is cheating on me with someone else the way he cheats on his wife with me.

I am angry with myself for expecting so much and then allowing myself to be let down. I am also angry that this woman who he calls his wife gets to live in the house that has the four cars and the dog. He's there with their kids giving her the security and support while I get to raise our child all by myself.

"There is no recognition that I am even the mother of your child and our daughter is a secret no one in your family knows about. You didn't bring any flowers to the hospital and you weren't even in the delivery room. No phone calls of congratulations and no visits to see how me and the baby were doing - as a matter of fact you only came to the hospital on the night that I delivered and that was it!"

I was in Grady hospital for three days since I had to have a C-Section. I was in excruciating pain and had to drive myself home because my mother had the missionary society conference and I didn't wanna call anyone else. Craig didn't answer his phone most of the time and when he did he said he couldn't get away. Now that I think about it, why would I still want to be with him after he treated me like that during the birth of our child?

Although she gets on my nerves, my mother spent the night with me in the hospital the first night and took care of my baby the second night. I just had to endure the bible scriptures from "Holier than thou Hattie" acting like I've committed murder by having a baby out of wedlock. If she knew that Craig was married she'd probably have a heart attack. She would never understand the love that Craig and I have because my father and her don't even sleep in the same room.

"I mean after three years and all that we've done together I meant so little to you that you couldn't even send flowers or come spend time with me? You didn't even hold your baby for the first eight days. I had to argue and curse at you and then all of a sudden you came over and spent some time with her."

"Alana, I'm trying but it seems like I can't get a word in edgewise. You're going to say what you want and feel the way you want no matter what I do. I will see you next week when I get back."

"Are you going to see me when you get back or are you going to just text me?"

"I love you girl and if I said I'm going to call you then that's what I'm going to do but you gotta stop working yourself up. Now stop crying! Clean up that pretty face of yours and put some clothes on that fine ass size two and get your work done."

Everything that he says to me is just what I need to hear and although I've had a horrible morning, the day will be a lot better knowing that my man loves me and gave me his word that he'll see me when he comes back. I still want him to leave his wife and I know that we need to still have our conversation when he returns.

One of my points of our discussion needs to be that Craig gives me some sort of payment each month to help out with everything that I need for this baby. There is no reason for me to keep doing everything by myself. Now because I'm nice, I'll only ask him for a thousand dollars per month; although I know he has much more. If he can afford to allow his spoiled ass wife to be a stay at home mom then he's able to afford me the same luxury. I have felt spiteful and thought about calling his wife and telling her about the baby just to hurt the both of them but that could backfire bringing them closer together against me.

Who knows maybe one day I will?

Nikki
"The Diva"

"Hey baby gurl, it's been real cool working in yo yard and all but it's getting late and I gotta go pick up my grandkids."

Mr. Evans was cool as ice and had more swagger than some of the so-called hippest and coolest young cats in the neighborhood. I made sure that I kept Mr. Evans' number as much as things around this house seemed to break down. I could always depend on good ole Mr. Evans to fix it and charge me in either beer, food or a check that he usually didn't cash. This day was different, seemed like he just wanted to sit around on the porch, sip lemonade and talk. Then there it was. The thing that every father that I meet seems to get around to saying,

"I want you to meet my son."

Mr. Evans kept going on and on about how wonderful his son Troy was and how Troy is a self made man, spiritual and hardworking. Of course, I didn't have to ask if he looked good because if he is a chip off the old block he probably is a Boris Kodjoe look-a-like. Or if he took after his father's complexion, more like Idris Elba.

Troy calls me as soon as I leave him a message. Now I'm starting to think *if he's all that, why is he single*? Why hasn't some woman snatched him up if he is so hardworking and fine? Why is he eligible? In my haste I forgot to ask Mr. Evans some really important questions about his golden boy. As I did with any of my other psychological problems or moral complexities, I got on the phone and called my counselor.

"Hey Mom! I am so sorry to bother you but I am really trying to understand what to do in this position?"

"What is it baby?"

The tone of her voice is always so comforting and soothing that I am assured that by the time I get off the phone, if she hasn't given me the answers to my questions, whatever the problem is it'll still be alright.

Mom I just really need to know what to do. Mr. Evans' son is meeting me at Café Blanche in an hour and I am petrified. Going out with Troy is my first real blind date. I have talked to him on the telephone but I don't know anything about him except the fact that he is the son of my handy man.

"Nikki, I'm never gonna get any grandkids if you keep sabotaging your chances. You have to take risks sometimes in hopes for a reward. Stop being afraid to meet new people and love again, Derrick is gone and it is way time for you to move on."

As much as I hate to admit it, my mother is always right. Derrick is gone and its time for me to stop being afraid to love again for fear that the next man will cheat on me. Hell, if it weren't for Derrick there wouldn't be a need for "The Diva."

I hate the very mention of his name. "Derrick Derrick Derrick!" The very sound of his name in my mind causes me to cringe. I loved him so much more than any man that I can think of in my short life-time but somehow he managed to take away from me what some people would call reason. I believed everything he said until even my own mother, who hardly ever interferes, had to tell me that I was running around with my nose wide open. The funny thing is, as much as I loved him, it just wasn't enough to keep him faithful.

Derrick was from Jamaica and I hate to stereotype but I think that it was something in his culture that said it was ok for a man to have several women all at the same time. He once told me that his father told him "Son, as long as you do your homework its ok to go out and play." Call me crazy but I think unfaithfulness was rooted in his genes and maybe that's why every time he looked me in my eyes and told me that he wasn't cheating on me, I believed him. Or every time he would come home late I would believe him. He would tell me that he was working late in order to make money for me and buy me something pretty.

Derrick is husky and tall just the way I like him. I couldn't believe the first time in the bedroom when that *Mandigo* took and picked my big ass up and slung me up against the wall. He had me like an officer; as a matter of fact I think he even told me to spread'em. Plus he wore a size 14 shoe! I have always been a bit of a freak but that man brought the best out of me. He knew how to spoil me and treated me better than any man that I knew. He was the first man that ever loved me for being a big woman and told me that he ain't never want me to lose weight. Imagine that! A man that loves double DD's and big booty! He was kind, generous, affectionate, and caring but he couldn't keep his dick to himself!

"What the hell??"

Why am I going down memory lane thinking about this nigga Derrick when I am supposed to be getting ready for Troy? Ok mirror, its time for the transformation. This man will know that I am Nikki "The Diva" with the reputation of being a man eater and if he even thinks about trying to play the game he playin with a real one.

I love the color red. It's just something about it that looks so good on my honey colored skin. When I turned fabulous and thirty I made sure to color my hair honey blonde so that if any little gray bastards popped up in my head they would immediately die a thirty-minute treatment death. I bought these bad-ass leather red boots from Macy's with the 4inch heel and a touch of mink fur on the side. This red sweater dress about two inches above the knee is gonna kill him softly as it hits every one of my fabulous curves. What's so good about it is that they had it in my size, sixteen.

My gurl Keisha tried her best to get this dress but her little ta ta's compared to my big jugs just didn't make it look right. When it was on Keisha it was pitiful, tight on the bottom and loose at the top. But for me, *honey-chile* please Jennifer Hudson wish she had these. My makeup is fierce. I try very hard to lightly accentuate the positive and gloss these thick lips so that they are kissable but don't look like I've been eating fried chicken. My curly blonde locks always make a statement as they flow. I wouldn't have it any other way and my stylist Raymone keeps my appointments every Friday for my phenomenal mane.

My millions of listeners on the radio wonder where all my confidence comes from but I see myself as two different people. First, there was Nicole Perry, you know that tried to be Derrick's wife, do anything for that nigga - stupid chic that I killed a long time ago. Now there is Nikki "The Diva" Radio unstoppable personality that exudes sexy on the microphone and is the poster child for all full figured women. I teach them the right way when they mama taught them the wrong way. The way to a man's heart is not through his stomach, it's directly through his chest and you better get them before they get you! Tear these heartless bastards up and tear they heart out or you will be somewhere crying and broke wishing you wouldn't have gotten that joint account, co-signed for a car, took out that loan for his business and helped him pay for a lawyer from his baby mama drama.

Okay! It doesn't take long to become fabulous so mirror, am I ready? "Hell yeah I'm ready! Hello Sexy Nikki. It's time to 'Get'em before you get got" so let's go eat some men!"

"Nikki?"

Oh my God this brotha is fine as hell! I done forget his name so I think I'll just call him '*cup of fine*'. Chocolate just the way I like'em and ooh wee it look like he work out underneath that sweater. I could just eat him up right now.

"Troy?"

I wanted to say Troy my boy toy but Imma try to keep it cool.

"How are you Sugar? Good to finally meet you."

When he smiled I almost fell over. I love black boys and green money. He smelled like *you know I'm fine* cologne when not shaking my hand but coming over to give me a hug. What a gentleman. He motioned me to sit and pushed my chair up for me.

"Its good to finally meet you to, seems like we've been talking on the phone forever."

My brain is gonna have to get my body under control because with every word of this man's deep tone, I feel my legs getting further and further apart. Stop it you whore your gonna have to stop this right now, but then I feel my hand under the table pull the dress from the waist down a little to expose even more of my 38DD cleavage. I make sure that with every joke he tells me that I giggle until my breast jiggle. Then I discreetly place my hand over my heart as to say *look at these.*

I don't play when it comes to food, and I don't care what a man may think about me. Salad is not my friend. I ordered the lobster tail with garlic mashed potatoes and spinach. I have this love affair with fresh bread although it doesn't love me back.

"You are so much prettier in person than your Internet picture Nikki, I really love your smile and your eyes."

Keep it up and Imma screw you. That's all I could think while his lying ass spewed all those beautiful.

Is he serious? Does he expect for me to believe that he is that into me when he just met me? Plus, as fine as he is I just know he's gotta be a ho. I was wondering why he is single at thirty-six and this fine? Well I guess I got my answer. He's a whore.

Most men are whores just like Derrick. They just want to love you and have you to take care of them and then find all kind of other women to take care of them. They don't know how to be faithful because they're just like dogs humping on everything they can find. You cook for them, clean for them, love on them, give them good sex and they move in pay your bills and buy you things while they screw Heather, Niecy and their ex named Trina. You even allowed him to coerce you into letting him on your radio show. Here I go drifting again.

Troy goes on "You are so classy and sexy; I'm really glad to finally meet you."

I eat and blah blah blah. This brown nosin nigga is really starting to get on my nerves. Doesn't he know that I have fans to kiss my ass and that I really don't need a boy posing as a man coming into my life just to kiss up to me. I need a man and not just any man, especially like this honey-talkin Negro. I need a real man! The one thing I can say about Derrick is that even though he may have been a two-timing no good liar, at least he knew how to take command.

"Oh my, look at the time. I have to get up for an early morning show tomorrow." Lying has never really worked for me but in this case, I have to get the hell away from this Negro before I go the hell off and tell him to shut the hell up.

"Ok pretty lady you make sure you go home and get your beauty rest - which won't be a wholc lot for you," he chuckles and opens my door for me.

Right when I was about to let him go I noticed the imprint on his wedding ring finger.

"So Troy did I ever ask you if you were married?"

He smiles at me thinking that I am asking for some relevant reason.

"No we didn't but that's easy. No I'm not married. As a matter of a fact I just got a divorce. Why do you ask?"

A wounded puppy! Mr. Troy Evans just became a little bit more appealing to me.

"Awwh Sugar that must have been devastating. Why don't you get in your car, follow me home and let's talk about it over a bottle of Henny."

There is no man that can resist the temptation of "The Diva". We went back to my house and in true Diva style I turned the tables and "talked" the hell out of Troy all night long.

"Nikki there is a gentleman on line one who says he needs to talk to you."

It's great having a job as a radio personality. This means that most places I go I get perks. Also, everybody knows "The Diva" and wherever I am is where they need to be. The only down turn is that for all the men that I sleep with and don't call back they know how to find me.

"Sugar, please take a message I'm on the air and if its not a caller bout the question of the day then please take a message."

Antoine is my gay boyfriend which means that he wants to be around me just so he can be in the fab lane. He is a diva in training for real but as far as being a personal assistant he has some work to do. I love his style, skills and he keeps me bling blinging and my phone ringing with bookings.

"Divaaaa he says that he is your brother and he needs to talk to you."

I think I just felt my heart drop into my throat. Why is my brother calling me? The only thing that I can think is that something has happen to my mother because my self-righteous, extra ordinarily perfect brother never calls me. I cursed him out when he told me that I was going to go to hell for living with Derrick. I don't care if he is a Pastor. When he feels compelled to judge me when he has his own dirty little secrets is when I have to take it there with him. You messing with the Diva now baby this ain't your little, chubby sister that you talked about like a dog when I was growing up. I'm grown and got my own show, my own house, my own car and millions of fans all around that love me.

I want so bad to tell my brother that as far as him telling me "living with Derrick is going to send you to hell" My response "I went to hell nigga and they told me I was to hot for'em so they sent me back." Marquis ass betta watch out because if he says the wrong thing he will get cursed out again.

"Hello Marquis, is everything alright with Mama?"

"Nicole yeah everything is fine with Mama the last time I checked. Why do you ask? Did you hear something that you are not telling me?"

This Negro here! Why does it always have to be somebody hiding something from him? He is sho nuff my daddy's child. Always thinking that somebody is doing something behind his back and not telling him what the real deal is. Can he for once just say hello and keep it moving from there?

"I was just asking Marquis because I don't hear from you unless something is wrong or you wanna tell me I'm wrong."

" I just called to let you know that I will be in Atlanta for a day or so visiting a friend of mine and wanted to see if we could possibly have lunch or dinner?"

My brother is in Atlanta and called me to meet me for lunch or dinner. Hmm, I don't know for sure but I smell something in the fire and it doesn't smell right. If there's one thing I know about my brother, it's the fact that he seeks opportunities for success like thirsty fools seek liquor. There is no way that he is in Atlanta and the only thing that he wants to do is have a dinner or lunch date with me. I am the most influential person on the radio in Atlanta and he has a roster of influential people that he calls on so he must want something.

"Ok I will give you over to Antoine and have him put you on my schedule for dinner." Seemingly excited Marquis said "Great I will see you then. God bless."

"Twan Sugar, where are all of my bikinis? I can't find anything."

I have been waiting all week to leave for my trip to Jamaica. Hedo is right up my alley as I have gone every single year for the past four years. Unfortunately, it's where I met Derrick. However; it's far away from the fame I have in Atlanta so I can do just about anything and get away with it. My reputation is starting to precede me *(laughing)*.

"Divaaaaaaa I found them Boo, you had them packed up in your Chanel bag."

Finally holding up my bikinis that were missing in action.

"Ooh chile, I wanna go. Honey you got all this pretty stuff packed up and you gonna have so much fun."

Antwan was the nosiest personal assistant that I have ever had but just as sweet as he can be. He always takes care of his Diva.

"Yep! And this time I got this fine sponsor slash sucker who is paying for the whole trip, putting us up in the most expensive hotel in Negril. The one time I've allowed him to get the goods he seemed to be a pretty good lay."

I wouldn't call him after we had our session in the back of my Escalade until he sent me them diamonds to the radio station and begged me to go on this trip with him.

"This dude is sprung and wants to be with me but Sugar Plum just don't know I'm the *"man-eater"* honey so as soon as we come back from our three day vacation, boyfriend is as good as gone!"

We both start laughing because Antwan already knows he's gonna have extra work screening the phone calls.

"How did your meeting with your brother go yesterday?"

I should have seen this coming. As I said before, Antwan is nosey but I can always trust him to keep quiet what needs to be quiet and boast what needs to be out. Bad publicity is better than no publicity at all and I can always count on the gay boys to support their Diva.

"This is hush hush Sugar but my older brother is thinking about branching out to Atlanta to pastor his own church."

Marquis sees the opportunities down here and wants to rub elbows with the black elite. He just wanted me to introduce him to some of the civil rights leaders and other powerful civic organizations and set up some meetings with them.

"If you ask me, he's just an opportunist but I guess it has paid off because some of the folks I made phone calls to already knew about him."

"If my father didn't teach us anything else before he died it was definitely how to "use whatever it is you got to get what you want."

Antwan smiles as he continues to rummage through all my expensive clothes and sniffing my perfumes. Sometimes I look at him and just wonder if the one woman he loved wouldn't have died in that tragic car crash, would he still be on the 'men who love women' team? It's a pity that this beautiful man inside and out has had to endure so much pain. Maybe it's why we vibe so well because he knows that with me he can be however he wants to be. Unlike my brother, I don't judge. Instead I just love.

"Diva your sponsor is on the phone honey!"

Finally this dude decides to call. He said he was going to call me an hour before the limo was to pick me up and our flight leaves in a couple of hours. I am a diva. I don't do waiting and they better have my liquor ready when I step into first class or else there may be hell to pay. Okay, I can let Antwan finish the packing while I light my cigarette and get into my sexy diva mood.

"Hello Craig. Okay…. yes I am ready, willing and waiting. I will have the doorman take the bags and see you in the car in bout an hour right? Ok Sugar see you then."

Lauren

Today is Tuesday October 13. I am starting a journal as advised by my counselor Dr. Michael Carson. I saw him for the first session yesterday Monday, October 12. I am seeing a counselor because my husband and I are getting a divorce. I can't tell anyone just in case we get back together again but after the fiasco in court I am losing hope. I keep thinking that this is a nightmare and eventually I am going to wake up. He left us on August 1st and when he left I didn't know anything about paying the bills or the location of any of our accounts. I am so hurt, I am unable to call him and since he has left before I just figured he would be back but that was not the case. This time he had been gone for two weeks! I can't possibly mention that my husband is gone to any one in the circles that I'm in because they would shun me.

So I just had a general conversation with a lady in the choir that I knew was going through a divorce.

"How are you holding up? How on Earth did you ever make it through your ordeal?"

I was all ears for the answer. She just felt the need to get things off her chest so she told me everything. I listened close to her every word and when she said that she was able to get spousal support before the divorce was final, I followed suit.

I was praying to God that I would not make my husband angry and that he would just come to his senses, simply come home, pay the bills or call me and tell me what I am supposed to do but he didn't. He knows all the little legal loop holes so instead of doing the right thing and to keep from paying me spousal support, he filed for divorce.

I just can't understand what I have done to make him want to leave me again and in dealing with this it has made me feel like I am going crazy. We went to court for the first time on October 5th. I am left feeling devastated, defeated and humiliated because the judge gave me nothing.

"Nothing! How can you give me and my children nothing?"

I was angry with my husband, his lawyer, my lawyer and God for what happened. My attorney sat there shaking more than I was, meanwhile the billionaire boys club consisting of my husband, his attorney friend and his judge friend decided my fate. "Lauren, I told you I am not the one to fight. You do what I say or you pay the consequences. I take care of everything and the children but because now you want to think for yourself you'll just need to get a job." I felt like a child in that little room listening to him scold me while everyone else including the Bailiff just watched me sit there in tears and take it. Wasn't I the one that worked at my father's company for three years while he went out and pursued his law degree? I now wish I would've taken Olivia's advice "Look here lil sis I'm telling you that every woman needs a stash. You listen to your pastor if you want to *talkin bout trust your spouse* and you will regret it later." Hindsight is always twenty-twenty. Instead I give all the money to my husband and let him take care of the bills because he convinced me he was the man and he needed to do it. I can't believe I was so busy being happy about shopping when I should've been learning about bills. His first wife told me that he was trifling but I couldn't see it because I was lonely and ready to be married. Wasn't it my parents that carried us while he was in law school and my father's connections that got him his first job? I really don't feel that he would pull a stunt like this is if my father was still alive. I have felt angry before but nothing ever like this. I now understand why people resort to violence.

It's Thanksgiving and now 3 months post Craig. Sometimes I cry but most days I just live from day to day feeling nothing. I still don't talk to anyone except for God and my counselor. Somehow, I convinced my mother to help with the kids saying that Craig is working more and I am volunteering more.

"Lauren where is your husband? It seems that every time I call he is always gone or out of the house. Is everything al right between the two of you? The kids are quiet and not really saying anything to me are you ok dear?"

My mother is always so concerned but her butting in would just make things worse.

"Oh mama you are a worry wart please; everything is fine. I am on the women's committee working towards Pastor's appreciation and did you know that I just received an award for volunteer of the year at the Crisis Center?"

I try to get her off the subject and it works at least for the time being.

This holiday is going to be hard for me. Unfortunately a couple of months ago I started collecting guys numbers just to have someone to call, but somehow I ended up getting physical with one of them and have been sleeping with him ever since. I don't even care about him but he feels like love and it takes my mind off of my husband for the moment. I am in emotional pain because of physical sin and I hate the way that I am. I never thought that it would be me in an adulterous affair. I just wish I could find my way back to the life that I used to have before I lose who I am entirely, but I don't know how.

Today is December 15th and it's freezing outside. I saw Craig today at the Bank. I know he saw me but we didn't say anything to each other although I wanted to say "Hi". He didn't look so great. He had on this blue hat, some old purple striped shirt, khaki pants and white socks with black shoes and for some reason it felt good to see him look so bad. I felt that God gave me that moment to see that he is just as miserable as I am. Just as I'm feeling good, I go into the credit union and the teller reveals to me that Craig has closed our joint account. "How can he do this without me signing for it? How are you just going to let him come in here and do something like this?" If only I knew what Craig had done before I let him slither away. Now I know why he didn't have the nerve or guts to say anything to me. "You

Coward!" I can't believe that he is doing this to me. If it weren't for the medication that this psychiatrist is giving me I know that I would be in my car right now following him to wherever it is that he is living and kill him! Maybe God is punishing me for the man that I slept with as if me not being able to have a child by my husband was not enough. What am I supposed to do now?

Today is Sunday December 23rd and I am really debating whether to go to church or not. We have our Christmas program and I know I am scheduled to usher. I used to love it now I hate seeing all the families come in with their smiling faces -especially the couples. I see them and reminisce on how happy I thought Craig and I were. Wondering, how did we go wrong?

When I was single, all I did was pray for a husband. I wanted a knight in shining armor to come and sweep me off my feet, rescue me from my father's house and take care of me. Having twins at sixteen did not give me a lot of options so I gave them up for adoption.

Craig was so perfect when I met him that I never told him about it. He treated me like no man had ever treated me before. He told me that he loved me and now I am learning from my doctor that although my father gave me material things, him never telling me that he loved me or showing affection had an effect on me. That dysfunction is what may have lead to the bad choices that I made and the rebellion as a teenager.

People think that wealthy people don't have problems and that somehow we are perfect. My mother and father should've gotten an Oscar for putting up appearances. When you look at all of their children, we are all messed up in one way or another.

My brother Andrew works on Wallstreet and although he takes deals, his addiction to cocaine has had a devastating affect on his family. To me it makes him no better than the crack whore on the corner. It doesn't matter that cocaine isn't crack, he's no better. My sister

Olivia is on husband number five and my younger brother Michael is now living as a transsexual name Michelle over in Paris somewhere. It's only a matter of time before she comes home and reveals herself to my mother now that Daddy is dead but I think she just doesn't want to hurt our mother. They were very close when she was a he.

I'm not going to church. They'll just have to understand. Now that I think about it I'm going through too much. I think I really need to make a phone call. Too much is going through my mind.

"Hello is Dr. Carson in today?"

Today is December 24th. I went to a Christmas fundraiser today and met Tikki Barber, a famous football player and took pictures with him. If I were still with Craig he never would have allowed me to go out and do that. I have not read the bible or prayed and now I am actually debating whether or not I'm ever going back to my church. How is it that when I was with Craig I was so overly holy and always going to church and now I can barely get up on Sunday. Ms. Hattie calls me all the time giving me more and more responsibility.

"Godmorning Sista Lauren I know its early but we gots ta get up when Jesus wake up and do what Jesus got for us to do. Sleep is for the weak and rest is for the weary! I am in need of you and Sista Jordan to call the florist and make sure the decorations are done for this Christmas fellowship. Can you do that for me Sista?"

I can never say no to Sister Hattie. She seems to know what's going on in my life even though I still haven't told anybody. Somehow, I am keeping up this lie very well. I always said that when I got saved I would never go back to the way that I used to be, now I wonder what have I become.

Today is January 1st. I didn't feel much like writing on Christmas but it was horrible, as it was the first without Craig. I have tried to find a support system for Julia and James but it is getting harder and harder to find people outside of our circle. They got gifts from the family that made them feel better. I sent them to be with relatives during the holidays as I sat quietly with the cat and cried through Christmas and New Year's Eve. My nanny called me and made up some excuse about getting another job. I think that her and Craig were sleeping together anyway. I am not in any kind of condition to make new friends but if I did, it would be with other women with children but its hard being married and single at the same time. I am uneasy in my mind and my spirit but I will try to pick up the bible and go to church this Sunday. I need to start the year off right.

Today is February 1st and I just got back from a wonderful women's retreat in the Blue Ridge Mountains. I was invited by Lillian, who has really been praying with me through the separation that I haven't told her about. . Lillian her husband, Craig and I were all friends before this separation and Lillian is about the only friend that I still have that has not turned away from me. I think that Craig told someone because so many have alienated me in our social clubs. Seems that they picked a *side and then realized that Craig is the more powerful so they went with him.*

The retreat was what I needed just when I needed it, for a moment I felt crazy being married but not having a husband. I got a fresh anointing and outlook on life because Pastor Brenda told me that she saw me as God sees me; dressed in white and beautiful. Another minister said that my footsteps were being ordered by the Lord. To think that at first I wasn't going to go because I couldn't find a sitter and then miraculously my mother called and decided to take a trip to Florida and take her grandchildren. I am not all the way healed but for the first time in months I can actually smile.

Today is February 14th and I was in a car accident. I don't know what is going on but I guess I just had a lot on my mind. I just recently got an executive assistant's job and was driving to work with tears in my eyes and looked up and ended up hitting the

back of a minivan. The guy got out and saw that there
was no damage to his car and looked at my face drenched
with tears and smeared mascara and was more concerned
about me than his car.

"Ma'am are you sure you're okay? Is there somebody you want me to call for you?"

I shook my head but deep on the inside I was screaming "HELP ME!"

"Well there is no damage to my car so I am not going to worry about it. You have a nice car what is this a ML 500?"

I knew he was just trying to start conversation to make me talk, smile or give some indication that I was not in shock. I just shook my head yes. The man then drove off and left with a concerned look on his face. I guess I should really thank God because I found out when I called the insurance carrier that my insurance was cancelled for non-payment. What a wonderful way to celebrate Valentines Day.

My whole day has just been one big mess from the phone call from my attorney to now being involved in an accident that scratched my front end. I don't understand how it is I can allow one little phone call to mess up my whole day but it did. I have been going through this divorce for months now and I am at a point where I don't even want Craig's ass back. I am so tired of him trying to be manipulative and controlling. Wasn't it him who left me because he felt that I was holding him back? He walks out the door after seven years of marriage leaving me with two children and tells me that its all my fault because I don't want more out of life.

Craig says he needs to pursue his dreams and I am holding him back. I put up with his silly arguments so he can have an excuse to go in the street and screw his whores. I put up with his misuse of our money and him talking about my weight and I even put up with his four day a week business trips. I am always there for him and always cared for him even when he slapped me. At the time I thought it was ok because my father used to hit my mother and my mother explained

that is was because she talked too much. Dr.
Carson has helped me to see that I accepted so
much emotional, verbal and physical abuse all for
the sake of having the security of a man.

Today is March 23rd. The lawyers set up a time
for my husband to come over and get the rest of his stuff.
I am so angry and can't believe that not only does he
leave me and rip my heart out of my chest but now he
wants to come to our home and tear it a part. He has
some nerve to take from here.

"Mr. Myers, how can you just let him do
this to me?"

Unfortunately my attorney is so wet
behind the ears that he can't even spell law.

After Craig left with half of my house and
I left the children with my mother I did what any
good loving caring wife would do – I went out
and screwed his brother! Uncle Al, as he is so
lovingly called by my children, has always been a
level-headed man and really has helped out a lot
with what the children and I have needed. He 's

been married for two years to Fredrica, a standoffish sort of woman.

I have known Al longer than his wife has known him. Al is beautiful inside and out and really didn't mean to enter my plan of betrayal. He just happened to be an innocent participant. I knew when I called him crying, he would come by.

"Hi Al, I am so sorry to call you like this" I made sure to sniffle every other word.

"It's no bother at all Lauren. I told you last time that you can call me anytime day or night. I hate that my brother and you are going through this but I believe that he will come out of this mid life crisis and come back home."

Some people say that Craig was going through a mid life crisis when he married me since I was only nineteen and he was thirty-five.

"Al, I am really needing you to come by. I just got a foreclosure notice from the attorneys that the house will be sold the first Tuesday of next month!"

"Oh my God Lauren why didn't you tell me earlier? You know I work at the Congressman's office. Your mother wouldn't help you? How can they foreclose, isn't the house in Craig's name?"

I didn't call Al to play two hundred questions. I just really needed to feel loved.

"Al, when your brother and I were married he was in bankruptcy. My father had connections and I was able to get the house in my name. My mother just lost her husband a year ago and the truth is that I haven't told her about Craig and I. I have always had someone take care of me and I need to finally grow up and do some things on my own."

"Ok I hear you, but first thing tomorrow I will get it rescinded so don't you worry about a thing. That being said, I'll be right over!"

Al came over and came to my rescue and once I leaned my head on his shoulder I knew he would hold me. Then I looked up at him with the tears in my eyes and said "take me" without opening my mouth. Al has always wanted me and even told me that if I was going to be a trophy wife I should have gone with the quarterback instead of the third string. I knew that night we would end up having sex and we did. I will never look at Uncle Al the same.

Today is April 7th. It's another beautiful Sunday morning and I am standing here contemplating how do I reconcile with God for what I have been doing with Al? How do I again stand at the doors of the church ushering with a smile on my face when I have fallen once again? I am trying to understand why it is that this morning I woke up not feeling anything. I am not mad at myself or Craig; nor am I hurt or maybe I am and have internalized it all so much adding another crazy notch to my resume. Maybe it won't come out right now. Maybe it won't come out at all, or maybe my emotions will explode while I am speaking to someone at my new job that Al got me, with my children or even at church.

Iesha

Earth, Wind and Fire singing *Loves Holiday* blasts through the radio as I catch myself bopping my neck back and forth and sliding across the kitchen floor in my terry cloth robe and fluffy blue house slippers while simultaneously cooking breakfast. I feel like springtime after winter, like a bird that has been set free.

The smell of bacon and eggs on the griddle and with every beat of "ba ba ba oughhhhh" I check the waffles to make sure they don't burn. My mind is clear and my body feels like it just had an oil change and lube job. The only thing missing was Jeheim. I wish he could've stayed in my bed last night after the good work that he did, *giving me somethin I could feel*. It was okay for him to leave at two-thirty in the morning and go back to his momma's house, especially since I sneak him in after my kids go to sleep. I was hoping and praying that the way he was giving it to me did not wake the kids. Then again, these kids sleep like bricks and since they

121

were upstairs in their rooms and I was in the basement's spare bedroom, I doubt very seriously that they heard anything.

It has been a long time since I had my legs up in the air and wrapped around a man's shoulders. I tried so hard to keep from making the sounds of passion but with every rhythmic stroke a moan came from deep down inside me. After about forty-five minutes of rocking steady, I guess I forgot were the hell I was.

"Hush baby yo kids gonna hear you"

Then as soon as he said that he gently put his hand over my mouth.

"Open yo eyes Esha I want to see those sexy green eyes."

I opened my eyes and looked deep into his and it was if I could see his soul - and it was beautiful. This Nigga is the truth! I could smell his cologne in my nostrils with the aroma like an aphrodisiac. The sweat beads were like race cars as they appeared on his forehead and then quickly ran down the side of his face. His goatee is perfectly trimmed and his deep chocolate skin is flawless. Now I'm even more turned on. I giggle and love looking into his eyes, they are so white and match his teeth. Making love to me makes him smile.

"Hush baby I know you almost there. Imma get you there!"

As soon as he lifted his hand from over my mouth he placed his index finger in his. Then he traveled to the tip of the deep south and stirred up the fire. With the juicy and passionate kiss of his luscious thick lips it triggered my body to shake uncontrollably. The last thing I saw was my light skin hands go bright as I squeezed all the blood out of them holding his shoulders so tight -finally downloading all my stress, anger, anxiety, fears, and worries.

"Shay, come on bring your brothers down. Yall need to eat before this food gets cold so we can go! I have to get dressed."

Although I love my lil midnight romps with Jaheim I pay for them in the morning. I knew I should have gotten up as soon as my clock went off but nawh I had to roll over and hit the snooze not once but two times. I am so tired I don't know what to do and this whole independent black women crap is so overrated. I swear that if I hear another song or rap about single black women and how powerful we are I am going to kill somebody.

It is hard as hell to wake up every morning at five to get three kids dressed. My youngest is Donte, who I affectionately call Man-Man. He's three years old and waking him up in the morning is like waking up a bear in hibernation. He could sleep through the second coming. My middle child is DJ who is seven and then there is Shayla, my eight year old who everybody says looks just like me.

Both of my older children wake up by their clocks but they sit in the bed for twenty minutes wrecking my nerves waiting on me to come in and scream at them like they don't have any sense. Thank God I always have these kids clothes ironed and ready or else I would be late.

"Shay did you spray yo hair with oil sheen?"

I usually wash and French braid Shay's hair on the weekends about every two weeks to have to keep from doing it in the mornings. Her stuff is too thick to be trying to do every morning. Not only did my first born get her daddy's complexion but she also got his hair.

"Yes Mama, I put it next to yo scrubs on the bed."

Oh my God why would that child put the oil sheen next to my uniform? I just hope the oil didn't get on my pants. I love working at the hospital and wearing a uniform everyday. It's so much easier to know that you are going to be wearing the same thing. I love to switch it up though. One day I have on blue with bright colored flowers the next may be yellow with happy faces, just depends on how I feel. Today I

feel like happy faces. I dash in the shower, get
out not bothering to put on any makeup, and thank
God that I have long enough hair to put in my
regular pony tail. I jump in my clogs, throw on
my scrubs, grab my babies and we dash out the
door.

"Good Morning Iesha!"

I can't stand my supervisor. She's an old,
tired ass dyke that every time she gets into it with
her girlfriend, comes to work with an attitude. I
can't wait until four o'clock comes so I can go get
my kids and head home. Seems like no matter
what happens at work, as soon as I see those three
crumb snatchers I smile.

"Good Morning Phyllis you look well this
morning."

In other words, she looks like she won't
have the same attitude today that she had
yesterday. I felt like I was living in pure hell
because although I love helping cancer patients,
it's hard to keep a smile on my face when Phyllis

is angry at her stud, making her micro manage everything we do.

"Iesha, Mrs. Kovan has been awaiting your arrival. She said that you are her favorite nurse and refuses to eat or cooperate with Clarissa."

In my mind I was thinking it's because Clarissa shouldn't even be working in nursing. I sometimes think the only reason that she got this job is because Phyllis likes Clarissa's lil tight wearing pant self, walking round here.

"Ok Phyllis I'm going to check in on her right now."

I got my first dose of satisfaction spending time at Mrs. Kovan's bedside. Before I could even get out of her room good, I spotted a beautiful dark skin Adonis. He has perfect dreadlocks to the small of his back about 6 ft tall with green scrubs. I notice his muscles as he rolls past me with a patient slowing down just enough to crack a smile at me with those beautiful white teeth reminding me why I am so happy this morning.

Grocery shopping is some straight bullcrap. I can't stand going to the store because it only reminds me of all the cooking I have to do and all the cocoa puffs, pizza snacks and juice boxes I gotta buy but can't eat. It's amazing what you see when you are shopping for a gallon of milk. I am strolling the aisles with my baby son tagging behind me and the only thing I see in front of me are other black women who look like me - single with kids.

I peep out their left hands as I am strolling through the aisles and as I count in my head it seems that the number of single black women can't even be counted on both my hands. I stop counting after ten and then the next thing I know I started counting white women. There seemed to be to many of them married to count. Now it could be that I am totally wrong about every woman without a ring being single. Maybe they just don't wear a ring or maybe they are wearing a ring and really just divorced, separated or living together with the infamous "shackin up."

Seems that the single black mothers in the grocery store all have the same look, especially when our kids are with us. It's a stressed look of *if this child ask me for one more thing Imma tear his lil ass up*, at the same time so focused as not to forget everything on the grocery list and count the money that we 're spending. We wear about 5 different hats in just one day and don't have time to be looking like we walking down the cat walk. We leave that to the single mama's out here lookin for a man at the grocery store or just single chics period. It's so funny to see them wearing four inch heels down aisle four strolling like they ain't got nowhere to go. Its funny to me cause the real single mama's be up in SuperMart with our gumshoes and sweats on with about two or three kids hangin off of us, a big purse to carry all the necessities like snacks, cell phone, coupons, grocery list, wallet, etc.

"Mommy I wanna candy"

This lil boy has asked me for candy from the time we got in the store and with my super mama skills I have somehow ignored the request but I think he is up to thirty-two.

"Man Man hush now I dun told you we gonna get you some candy if you good. You gonna be good for Mama?"

This lil boy is a spittin image of his daddy, which is probably why I spoil him so much. I love all my kids but Man Man with his fat cheeks and dimples knows how to grab my heart. All I can do is look at him and smile but I know good and hell well he's not getting no candy! Why? So he can drive me and my last nerve crazy? Mama loves you my lil BooBoo but you ain't getting no candy goes straight through my head. Instead I reach in my pocket and hand him my cell phone to play with after I place it on lock. I need to hurry up and get out of this grocery store so I can pick Shayla up from her dance class and then take D.J to basketball practice.

There is a full moon out tonight and the sky is so clear that it seems like the stars are 5 feet above my head instead of millions of miles away. Finally it's quiet in the house; hell it should be its almost midnight and I have to go to work in the morning. Here lately I have been so tired and stressed that Dr. Anderson prescribed me anxiety medication saying that, "Ms. Johnson you really need to get some rest." If it were that easy don't he know that I would but if I stop, who is going to take care of these kids, get these bills paid, fix this house, and everything else that needs to be done? Then suddenly while sitting out here on my porch, as peaceful and quiet as it is, a cool breeze blew and felt like the breath of God that I needed to fill me up. I don't know why but at that moment I felt a tear come down my face. The breeze, the moon, the porch all reminded me of times that I spent with Darius and how sometimes after spending time talking on the porch we would go to our bedroom and make love. I couldn't help but think of him as my stomach continued to cramp because he was the one who would make my tea and put honey in it just the way I liked it. Although I shouldn't feel this way it's hard for me not to cry wondering if I will be by myself forever until I die.

I hate so much feeling like if I get sick, who is going to be there to take care of me when I have no good prospects and my family lives so far away – intentionally? "Hey Iesha" I finally had to answer the phone as Alana been calling me all day. "It's cousin D's anniversary so I wanted to check on you. How are you?" "I am a good woman and have so much to offer but this whole dating scene is hard and having three children doesn't make it any easier, especially since I'm not about to allow my kids to see mommy having all kinds of different "uncles" in and out of the house. My heart hurts and it is starting to cause my body to ache trying to get over Darius's death only a 1 year ago today. It's hard for me to move on when I don't understand why God took him from me."

Darius and I had our differences and its true we argued like cats and dogs but at least I knew that I had someone to come home to even if we weren't married. Talking to Alana was free therapy because she was a lil dingy but a good listener. "I mean we were gonna get married eventually. I was with him for almost 7 years. It was good enough for me, but I loved my kids too much for it to have been good enough for them." Not being married was the subject of most of our arguments. "I know when I went to church the pastor preached about not shacking up and not fornicating but right now depressed is the only feeling that I feel and bills are what I need paid so Jesus will have to just forgive me." Alana had her own issues so I knew she wouldn't judge me. I desperately want someone here with me right now to share this tranquil moment and hold me and tell me its ok. "I feel like I am going to go crazy trying to do all of this by myself and no one in my corner and no one on my team. It's cool for Jaheim to come over, do me and take me out from time to time but I ain't trying to have no nigga come shack up with me and my kids again." I seem to have a different guy to do different things but I can't find one that does everything. Like, Jeheim is great when I need affection, Mike is great when I need something fixed, James is so sweet and I can talk to him about anything and then there's Reggie. Unfortunately they are all great guys and they all truly care about me but none of them can compare to Darius. I talk to Alana a lil more then hang up to go to bed.

I can't keep doing this running up the stairs to answer the phone crap "hey gurl just checking up to see how you doing" she has a simple ass voice and makes me sick to talk to her but she is my brother's wife. "Hey T.T. I'm fine just keeping my head above water and taking care of these kids" I always keep things short with her because I don't want to give her any ammunition to carry back and gossip with. Most of my family has talked about me so bad that I refuse go around them and pray they don't come around me. This is one of the reasons why I moved six hours away. Finally, the phone rings and I have to get the other line. "Sorry T.T. I gotta get my other line I'll have to call you back." Click "Hello, hey Reggie where you at?" Good Ole Reggie. "Baby I'm about ten minutes from your house. Make sure you open the garage so I can pull my car in" a brand new black on black Mercedes which I will gladly deposit in my garage and later on this evening make a Reggie withdrawal.

Gena "Ginger Snaps" Baby

I am lonely. I am laying face down across my bed armed with a notepad and pen to scribble away my pain, although it's hard to write and see when your eyes are full of tears. With every stroke of this pen I write my deepest heart and somehow its like therapy yet cost so much less than I charge my clients:

Hope is running low my mind is cloudy not clear
Thoughts of when and how long before you appear
Intimacy comforting me strong shield of protection
6 foot two filled with love and affection
forgiving kind family oriented not tainted by society
charismatic orgasmic intellectual who takes control
takes the pain away rainy days we lay loves me from the pit of his soul.
Waiting patiently is getting the best of me and starting

To take its toll starting to become emotional or
sometimes
Feeling numb unable to understand why this man
has not
Come. Its alarming why prince charming seems to
be
Fleeing from me or is it that I just cant see who is
to be
Maybe already in front of me. I shout out to the
God
That I have completed all his task whatever He
has
Asked and all I want in return why would the
father
Allow me to burn. Please answer me I'm crying
Wholeheartedly heart is faint complaints unable
to
Feel anymore always looking at the opening door
Wondering if this is possibly the day when he will
see
Me and transcend how I feel about men. How I lie
when

I say yeah I love myself don't need nobody else when

I know that I do just mad cause I aint got no boo.
Independence is overrated getting on my nerves if
I hear another word about strong black women
I feel my wimp a comin asking with my eyes for
Him to take this strife out of my life and make me his

Wife. And allow me to put the multiplicity into his
Vision and dreams allow me to bring the peace and love
That he never thought of. So much deep inside of me

Long suffering long-suffering long-suffering. Lord
Deliver me hope is fading far from me Hope is running
Low my mind is cloudy not clear Thoughts of when and
how long before you appear.

Writing is always my solace and what's funny is that whenever I read my emails of the accolades of so many of my adoring fans they say that my books or blogs inspire them to write. Its amazing to me that I found my true gift and passion in what God has for me to do. I love this writing but the loneliness I don't feel that I deserve. It's so hard for me to be human to my fans.

"Why the hell is the phone ringing at 3'oclock in the morning?" I roll over to look at the clock. I fell asleep again in my clothes with pen in hand. "Damn, I just missed it!" Here I go, contemplating on whether I should do the responsible thing and listen to the message or just let it go. "It may be some money." I go checking voicemail: *"you have one message" "the following message was received at 3:10am"* I can't believe this trick is calling me at 3'oclock in the morning and it can only be one person – Angel. "Hey Ginger Snaps Baby this is Angel just calling to remind you of the gig today at 2pm, Bellame Park 14th Annual Jazz Festival I will make sure that Lou picks you up on time and the band is set up. Love you Bye."

"This chic is crazy! I can't believe that I actually slept with her!" I am really starting to rethink this whole bisexual thing. She starts out as my protégé and ends up part of my ménage à trois. These are booty call hours! What am I doing still allowing her to be around me? I am not bisexual, I am a life coach and I need to practice what I teach. Keeping her around is just a temptation for me. She is young with perky size 36C breast and a tight round cute ass - all the things that I desire to be including the fact that she has the privilege of being light skinned with pretty hair.

Angel's mama is from Brazil and her daddy was some famous black football star who is now a *"has been"* still trying to share the lime light with the young guys faking the funk as a coach. I met with Angel's mother Renata several times as her life coach to get her through her husband's constant insults. Angel's mom was so impressed with me and noticed that I needed a personal assistant and offered up her daughter *"the groupie gone wild."* I wonder what Ms. Beaumont would think if she knew I was doing her daughter.

Most of my clients have these extraordinary issues or problems that they need to keep top secret because of their celebrity or social status. I am rated number one among the elite after being on the number one female talk show in the nation. My book sales and bookings as a jazz artist soared. At first, this was just a way for me to work through my own personal pain from the past and now it has become a lucrative profession. Unfortunately, it comes with groupies and most of them are women with problems. I am not really bisexual. I love men and if the right man came along I'd be on him in a heart beat, but men don't seem to want me. I feel it's because I am a dark chocolate sista, with dreadlocks who will not settle for just any man. Most of them look at me

and my success and automatically assume that I
already have a man or they are intimidated by me.

I can't surround myself with all these men
because I have an image and reputation to protect
and that's my money. I have standards and will
not go for a man that wants to move in with me,
sleep with other women while sleeping with me or
just can't commit. I see it when I go to most of
the clubs to perform. There are these sized 1,
young light skinned black females with either
silky straight hair down their backs or some form
of French refined weave. Those are the ones that
most of the men surround, buy drinks for, or ask
out. I see it all throughout the magazines and the
front covers are always doused with the light skin
women whose makeup is made to make them look
like they are white. I don't think that I have ever
seen a dark skin sista with locks or a nappy fro on
the cover of Essence, Ebony or Jet and they are
black magazines.

I have felt racism from my own people
since I was a child. My aunts would take my

sisters and I and treat us all differently. My sister
Melba who is very fair and had a head full of
curly hair would always get to stay up late or got
bought new dresses because her father was white.
My father on the other hand, although my mother
loved him dearly, was a dark skin Negro who
worked himself to the grave trying to make ends
meet. My aunts and grandparents never asked me
how I felt about his death nor did they buy me
gifts to get me through it but Melba was always
babied and even told right in front of me that she
was the prettier sister.

Anyway, My first book *"Ginger Snaps
Baby"* (which is also my stage name) is a book
about dark skinned women. I feel rejected but I
can't get hung up on why men don't stay around
and love me. Instead I get my release by writing
books about why and how a woman should
empower herself. Statistics show that my dark
skin sistas support me the most and as a result,
their support has made me rich. Meanwhile, in
my natural craving for human affection and

someone to love I just so happen to sleep with a woman. I don't love Angel nor do I ever see myself living with her, walking hand in hand or any of the other lesbian attributes but she serves her purpose.

Ring, Ring, Ring. "What the hell? I feel asleep again. Who the hell is at the door?" I look over at the clock and now instead of the 3am hour its 9:27am. "Who is it?" I love the whole intercom thing. I never had something like this growing up. "It's Zora wake up!" Zora and I have been friends for a very long time but I will never tell her about what I do in my private life with Angel or any other woman. The men I always tell her about but the women must remain my secret because as much as she loves me as a friend, I just don't feel that she would completely understand. I'm dragging this morning going to the door. "Hey gurl what you up to?" This whole poppin up over to the crib thing with Zora is really gonna have to stop. "Hold on Zora I will let you in just wait one second." I have to hurry up and get myself together or else she will see that I had a pity party and slept in my clothes and will start feeling sorry for me. I won't allow her to do that. "Good morning Z you want some coffee or something?" I am still sluggish as I walk around in these pitiful ass, leopard house shoes and zebra housecoat that do not match. "Ha ha ha Ginger what the hell you got on? You must have had a long night at the club?"

Zora is always so happy and so damn loud in the morning. And when she laughs she so big that she reminds me of Santa Claus - just a big, fat, happy, jolly white girl. We met at the Acid Baby Festival in New York and had so much in common. When I found out that her husband Robby played the bass guitar I knew instantly that we would be friends. We are so close that she named her daughter Ginger Zoe McNeil. Robby is my lead guitarist for my Jazz Band Mahogany Soul. "You know what Zora, I'm actually glad that you dropped by I've got a lot of stuff I gotta get together for the book tour." "Ok Gin that's cool but I really wanted to know how is that new client that I sent over to you working out?" Zora is very influential. She started her publishing company after authoring 27 books with four of them being on the Best Sellers List. She referred me to Renee Colbert, a big time marketing giant who has been a client of mine for about four months now. "Zora she is fine but you know that I can't talk about her situation with your nosey self." "Ha Ha Ha I knew that sista needed some guidance. Her energy is so negative. Okay let's get to it, what do you need for me to do?"

The smoke from the incense fills the room and as soon as I enter in, the mellow grooves from the saxophonist are like honey to my eardrums. I love Verge' it's the creative club in Detroit that I go to when I just want to hear some good music. Tonight my favorite band *Fusion* is playing and the lead singer Cocoa gave me a ticket to see her sing. Cocoa is beautiful. I first saw her at this jazz in the park thing I featured at last summer. She was wearing a white sundress and her hair was long and wild. The wind had it blowing everywhere but that girl could sing. She was singing this old song called "band of gold" and she was blowing it out the water. Crowds were surrounding her like she was giving away free food but I guess her music is like food to the soul.

Cocoa and Fusion are so hot that they are featuring tonight and have brought out some of the heavy hitters in the music industry. The tickets to get into Verage' are usually $10 but tonight they are $20 and the place is packed. As soon as I walk in I feel the heat as if being 98 degrees outside was not enough. This place reminds me of a high-class juke joint that sat way back in the cut. It had the most eclectic pieces for decoration and was designed on the inside like it came straight out of architectural digest. The artwork that surrounds the room is tastefully done especially since the owner's son is the artist. All of a sudden I hear my name come over the mic "Give it up for Ginger Snaps Baby in the house!" I can't believe Miko little Asian butt just hollered my name over the mic, I was trying to be discreet coming in here. Now here it comes, the beautiful but sometimes bothersome fans that want my autograph. "Hi Ms. Snaps I love your work can I please get a picture with you? I saw you when you came to London!" "GSB please look this way!" Immediately, Big Teddy (my bodyguard) takes me to the back where I can actually enjoy the show without being mobbed. Oh, and Angel is tagging somewhere behind. "Wow, Ms. Gin are you ok?" Angel is always so surprised at the adoring fans and concerned with it's affect on me when after 10 years in the game I am used to this. "You know what Sweetie Pie, I am feeling a lil wound up why don't you roll up mama one of them trees." I knew there was a reason I keep Angel around she's easy on the eyes, rolls my joints to perfection and she's a great P.A.L. "Gin isn't this room nice? I love the candles and the smell. They have your water, fruit and the privacy we requested. Anything else you need?" She hands me the well rolled 1inch leaning over just enough for me to see her hanging cleavage and shapely form under her sundress in this low lit room. Angel has been crying for attention since I haven't touched her since our last encounter 7 months ago. I think it makes her work harder for me although I have repaid the favor by getting her a modeling contract for Mac makeup. "You know what Angel, I'll have another Hairy Navel but I want you to make it because you know just how I like it." "Ok Gin, I will go and bring it right up." I will cleanse my spirit with herbs and oils tomorrow but I really want to enjoy myself tonight.

Finally Cocoa goes on and she starts singing this new song and the words are getting to me:

COME ON!
LEFTYOUR LEFT YOUR LEFT YOUR LEFT RIGHT LEFT
CAN YOU KEEP UP
WORK THAT BODY WORK THAT BODY BABY COME AND GET THIS BODY WHAT YOU GONNA DO BABY WIT THIS HOTTIE WHAT YOU GONNA DO BABY

WIT THIS BODY GRIP MY BODY TILT MY BODY
FLIP MY BODY WHIP THIS HOTTIE KISS ME BABY
FLIP ME OVER TAKE ME BABY AS YOUR LOVER
WHAT YOU GONNA DO BABY WIT THIS BODY
WHAT YOU GONNA DO BABY WIT THIS HOTTIE
CAN YOU KEEP UP UP CAN YOU KEEP UP UP CAN
YOU KEEP UP UP CAN YOU KEEP CAN YOU KEEP
NOW BREATHE AND BREATHE COME ON
SECOND ROUND
TAKE THAT LOTION GET ME BABY MAKE
THE MOTION WIT ME BABY WHAT YOU GONNA DO
BABY WIT THIS BODY WHAT YOU GONNA DO BABY
WIT THIS HOTTIE TAKE YOUR HANDS AND GRAP
MY HAIR BABY TAKE ME EVERYWHERE
SLAP MY BODY WHIP MY BODY GRIP MY
BODY GET THIS BODY

She comes off stage after her set and heads straight to my VIP suite. "Hey Ginger! I am so sorry about Miko blabbing he was just so excited to see you come and so am I." She smells like frankincense and her body is glistening from giving her all on the stage. I am trying to focus and keep my friendship with Cocoa but I sometimes wonder if I was attracted to her

151

because of her talent or because she is so beautiful. Her eyes are like big balls of light because she has a lovely soul. Her skin is so smooth and just like her name, carries the tone of cocoa butter. And although I am not trying to add drama to my life by being with another woman, this one may be inevitable. "Thanks for having me. You did so well and its okay, I love my fans." I calmly exclaim but then she leans over to hug me and because she is so natural and doesn't wear a bra, I feel all of her. She then adds to my temptation when she kisses me on the cheek. She is young and full of energy. I think she's at least twenty-one. I know that she can have any man in this place especially since she already has all of their attention. "Gin I have your drink." Oh hell, I can tell by the way that she looked at Cocoa and the tone that she used when she said *drink*, that there may be some issues. I'm high and feeling good so se rah se rah. "Thanks Angel, you know Cocoa right?" She nods her head and pounds on the I-Pad like she is crazy.

The night goes on with me introducing Cocoa to people that I know and her introducing me to people that she knows but the one person that we both know is Billy "Beatz" Bloomberg. Beatz and I go way back when he was rocking the guitar with a band called Fuzz. In the early 90's he saved up his money and started a record label and now he has some of the hottest artist in the world. Beatz was impressed with Cocoa and Fusion and now she will finally get the backing she deserves!

"I am so excited Ginger. I finally get to go to Beatz studio and I owe it all to you. I'm so happy. Come on let's go celebrate!" As soon as she says that my very competent but jealous assistant Angel says "Ginger you have a flight to Atlanta first thing in the morning." I must say it's kinda cute seeing her act jealous but my flight is at 10am and I know that this will be worth it. "Thanks Angel but I'll get up and when you come to wake me in the morning can you have a herbal tea and that special black soap in the room."

Sending Angel home and taking a different limo was not hard for me since this is what I do all the time. I have told her not to get attached and that it was only sex but for some reason, she can't seem to understand.

Going out on the town with Cocoa and Fusion was awesome but wine and me don't mix so getting twisted beyond repair was the color that I was wearing. "You should stay with me Ginger I really don't think you should go home like this" If only she knew that those were words that I wanted to hear. After saying goodbye to the band and going in the house Cocoa called her boyfriend Mike and had a long conversation while I tried to sober up in the shower.

Her studio apartment is not big enough for a whole lot of furniture so after she ate her usual 2am captain crunch cereal she told me I could share the bed with her. The liquor possessed my body but my mind was still clear and all I could do is lust for her as she slid in the bed with a little pink nightgown and no panties on. I pretended to

154

be asleep and by this time it was probably around 3:30am when I peeked under the cover and notice her gown slightly lifted above her hips. Since I knew that I could always blame my actions on the liquor I wrapped my arm around her and pulled myself close allowing my naked skin to touch hers. My hands begin to have a mind of there own as I touched her between her legs and when she woke I had already had my mouth on her breast. I then lifted my gown and offered her mine when she said "Ginger I've never done this before" but her actions throughout the night said different.

Hattie

"Thank you Lord, I am grateful to God to have a husband in a sinful world full of sad single women." I'm a lil stiff this morntin but I will give thanks ta God evry morntin I wakes up.

I know that I am under spiritual attack but the devil ain't got no new tricks I sees what he doin. I had a dream last night about my husband's friend Bo. *In the dream I was on the phone and my grandbabies was in the living room watching TV. I went to open the front door, Bo was there, and because I know him, I let him in. I started walking to the kitchen and when I felt the presence of somebody else in the house, I turned around and there were about four other men in the house. They was great big ole men with huge muscles. I told them to get out and when I did that, my grandbabies disappeared. One of the men slammed the front door real hard behind him. The next thing I know I was trying to get to the bedroom to call for help when Bo followed me and tied me up with one of my brassieres. I tried*

157

to fight the men but they was to big and strong so
I felt powerless against them. The next thing I
know one of the men had ripped off my housecoat
and was having his way with me. He was puttin
his hands on my breastes and opening my legs
they each took a turn and then it was Bo's turn.
When the dream was over I woke up and was
lying in a puddle of wetness in my bed. It was
3'oclock in the morning and although I would
love to have had relations wit my husband, I knew
that John wouldn't touch me. So I got up, walked
quietly pass his bedroom, cleaned myself up and
went back to sleep til it was time for our women's
prayer call at 6 o'clock in the morning.

"Now Ms. Hattie what is your blood
pressure doing this high? You cooked one of
those big Sunday dinners again didn't you?" I
always smile and look up in shame because this lil
girl be tellin it like it is. Whenever I have a doctor
appointment on Monday my blood pressure be
high and my nurse Iesha be on me about it.

That's one of the reasons I try not to make a
Monday appointment because I know I'm wrong
and she right but I got stuff to do. "Ms. Hattie
your birthday is only four weeks away and I want
to see you reach 60." I know she loves me and try
to change the subject. "You know they gonna
have this big birthday party for me at the church.
It's supposed to be a surprise but chile they can't
keep nothing from me. I'm from the ole school. I
know everything, I see everything and I hear
everything. Plus, it pays to be over the Women's
organization cause you know we women can't
keep nothing secret. Sista Lola told me about it
over a month ago."

Iesha went to just laughing til she forgot
about how high my pressure was. It give me joy
to see her laughing, especially since I know what
she den been through. I think it was last year
around this time when those babies daddy got
killed in that motorcycle accident. When I didn't
see her for my appointment I asked about her and
the doctor told me what happened. I ain't waste

no time finding out where she lived so me and my prayer warriors Sista Lola and Francine could go and take care of her. That girl was laid up in the bed, house a wreck, with some lil young girl trying to cook but burning a boiled egg. It took us bout a week or so to pray her through til she could get out the bed and start living again. "The devil ain't got no new tricks" God got a plan for this girl's life cause she good to everybody. "So Esha have you started dating again? You young and pretty thing, it's time for you to get somebody." She looks at me with her smile looking like a sweet angel. I know she doin something with somebody cause for the past couple weeks she been beaming like new money and bouncing round here like a baby in a sugar shack. "Ok Ms. Hattie, me and you have already had this conversation and I just don't feel like I'm ready to get into a serious relationship right now. Plus I got three kids to think about and they come first. I don't have time for a man. You and your husband have a perfect marriage but it's not the same nowadays." Did she just say she don't have time for a man?

These young women kill me when they hurt and don't wanna admit it. They say they ain't got time when the real deal is they just don't wanna put they self out there. "Yes baby me and you dun talked and I think its some good men that wanted to take you out but honey you be shuttin'em down before they get in the door good. Just give a man a chance to love you cause it's plenty of good men out here that want a good woman." She saw a picture of my baby son Julian and I reluctantly introduced the two of them but I really don't want him to have to take on the responsibility of three kids. As God would have it, they didn't make no love connection. Iesha came back saying that Julian and her went shoe shopping and would now be the best of friends while he came back talking about she just wasn't his type.

"Ok Ms. Hattie I got all your vitals. It's time for your treatment now, but Imma give the doctor your chart and he may want to see you first. Oh and I heard what you said and I'm going to seriously take it under consideration. Giving a man a try." Thank God somebody's chile is listening to me. Lord knows mine don't.

As a young woman, my mother gave me nothing about men since she had only been with my father, the Reverend L.C. Jackson Sr. of the Mt. Zion Missionary Baptist Church in Alabama. For some reason, even with their example, I Hattie Mae McKoy formally Jackson have failed in my marriage. I will continue to pray and tell the devil that he is a liar! My good book say "The fervent effectual prayer of the righteous availeth much." I aint gonna let the devil have my husband because I know that it was God that gave me to this man and John is a good man. I knew we was getting married when I met him. I was a young beautiful five foot five, caramel skinned, brown-eyed daughter of a very well respected preacher. My father would say from the pulpit "Say it, see it and believe it". People's lives were being changed and he became well known all over the South.

While my father traveled all over the South, me, mama and my fourteen brothers and sisters were left alone at home. I ain't never wanted a lot but the only thing I longed for was a man to love and take care of me. In today's world you have these independent women but I'm from the old school. I wasn't afraid to stand up and say "I want a man to take care of me". Then it finally happen after all of my Mr. Wrongs, God gave me Mr. Right also known as John Alan McCoy, when I was at the ripe age of twenty-two. Before John, there had been a slew of men but I wasn't about to tell John that. Neither mama, daddy, or any church members knew but I decided that I could no longer continue to be used and abused. I decided to pray and started trying to live like a good church girl.

I kept my mind off boys by doing what they call " putting a lot of pots on my stove" or keeping busy. My hot tail joined almost every committee in the church as if I wasn't already on enough. Then somewhere in the middle of keeping busy at church and trying to be a good girl I met John. I was invited by my girlfriend Cookie to a Saturday afternoon bar-b- cue when this tall, dark skinned, brother with jet black hair and rippling muscles walked up to me "my dear I must have your name or I think I might just die." John was square with the line, but at first sight he reminded me of a "Shaft" look a like, and all the girls wanted him but he wanted me. We been married now 37 years and I keeps praying that John will one day touch me again.

"What am I going to do Cookie? There are some things that never get old, money, me and my sista girl friend Cookie. At the age of fifty-four I could not believe that I was diagnosed with breast cancer so after talking with the Lord the next person I called was Cookie. "We gonna get through this Pea", she always call me Pea cause my mama would make me sit out on the porch and pick peas. I loved picking and cooking peas for everybody with smoked neck bones and hot water cornbread. Cookie and I grew up right down the road from each other and when John took a job close to Atlanta, Cookie and her husband Fred helped us move. Like I always say "the devil ain't got no new tricks" sure nuff after Cookie and I prayed and I took some of those chemo treatments, the next time I went to the doctor they couldn't find a trace of cancer.

John moved out of our bedroom not to long after I got sick cause I couldn't do my wifely duties. I ain't feel bad about it. I just feel like it was the Lord telling me that I need to thank him for giving me back my life and concentrate on church. I gave John these babies and take care of him while he be working and I cook for him but the church needed me to come in there and get it shaped up. I am over several committees and Pastor Miller tell me all the time how she don't know what she would do without me. I raise my children the best I could and if they don't wanna listen I got to do what the good book say and "loose them and set them free." I give them to God because Troy, Julian and Alana is all grown. I don't have time for they foolishness getting my pressure up. I see John now when we pass each other in the house and I give him his supper but he ain't never been a man that come to church. I just feel I failed because I must not have prayed enough for him or else this cancer wouldn't have come back.

"Hattie Mae!" I keep telling him that when I am in my prayer time that he don't need to bother me but when John get in his drink he forget. "Yes Sir?" I already know what he want his supper but I got to pray with Sista Esther. Her husband is sick in the hospital and she was one of my prayer partners early on before they left the church to move to Arizona. Everyone in the community sees our house and come over and tell me that John and me are the perfect couple. Some people said that if they looked up marriage in the dictionary a picture of me and John would be there. I ain't never left because John is a good provider. He takes care of home. I knew about the outside child that John had and with God was able to get over it and move on with my marriage. I forgave him and we have given Ty Quesha's mama money for that chile from day one but it aint nobody else's business what go on in this house or in this marriage. If only the wives of today knew how to keep they mouth shut and handle they business and be satisfied.

"Hattie you gonna be alright" Cookie's calming voice brings me out of my daze. "Every time he get in his drink he go to acting like this. Lord I am tired and I he getting to old for this." I can only cry uncontrollably. The pain is just too great to bear and I am too old and tired to start the dating game again. Besides, whose going to want a fifty-nine year old woman with no education and no job? "Fred talked to John and he is coming home Hattie. He says that he loves you and he is coming home." Home thank God he is going to come back home. I hear Cookie talking and trying so hard to console me and I really thank her for it but if only she knew. My soul has died. I walk, move and breathe but there is no life in me. This time the cancer is winning.

 "Good morning Pastor Miller, its time for you to wake up. Is there anything you need this morning?" "Good morning Sista Hattie. Is there something wrong?" I had to get use to the whole idea of having a woman as a pastor but Pastor Miller has done a wonderful job. I am proud to call her my pastor. She really loves the people and has grown the church, put us on television and was asked by the Mayor of the city to do the inaugural prayer. She also got a discerning spirit. "Oh Pastor I'm just a lil slow this morning but I'm going to make sure that the sisters get you what you need. I plan on making Sunday dinner but I may have to miss 7:45 service if the Lord don't take these molasses out my feet." God know, Pastor and the doctor but it ain't no reason for nobody else to know about this cancer. The doctor say it den came back and is spread all over but "the devil ain't got no new tricks" I still

believe if the Lord want to he can heal me. "Ok
Sista Hattie the Lord may just be telling you to go
ahead and stay in bed this Sunday. I think the
Lord gives us grace and mercy especially for a
member like you that never misses a Sunday or
Monday through Friday if you want to put it that
way."

Pastor Miller joking with me was just what
I needed this morning after dealing with John
getting in his drink last night. Then the devil
jumped into my eldest chile Troy when he come
over here lying on my baby son. "Mama Julian is
a faggot. He ain't never gonna give you no
grandchildren! I am sick of coming over here
helping you find Dad and when you call Julian he
partying or out and about and you accept it. I have
a life to and I try to do right but you make excuses
for "Mr. Downlow pretty boy" and he don't never
help you." My head was hurting to much last
night to hear that but I know that it's because
Troy's jealous of his brother that he say that type
of stuff about him. Julian was a pretty baby when

he was born with a head full of curly hair. The
neighbors all talked about how pretty he was
because him and Lana came out looking like my
side of the family. My side got Indian in us while
Troy take after my husband side and they much
darker wit that bad hair. The girls have always
been after Julian but he just real picky. It don't
mean he funny. Troy just gonna have to get over
it and realize he the eldest and he gotta help. My
baby, Alana just had a baby so she can't help
nobody do nothing right now and she call me the
other day wrecking my last nerve asking me to
keep the baby while she go to a party. "Hattie
Mae!" Lord here go this man calling me now. I
know it's early in the morning and John ain't
drunk no more. "John Imma getcho breakfast. I
told you I was on the phone with Pastor." Oh
Lord now here come this fool walking down the
steps. I can always here him a mile away because
no matter how he fix them steps it's always that
one at the bottom that squeak. "Hattie, I gotta get
over to Mr. Johnson house I told him I be there by

7am to finish painting. I needs my breakfast so I can go." "John I dun told you Imma fix yo breakfast. I just got off the phone with Pastor. Now I gotta warm these greens and macaroni and cheese up for Sunday dinner." I'm opening the cabinets and slamming pots and pans and I can't seem to catch my breath but Imma make this man his breakfast for he get on my last nerve. This headache is really bothering me. I gotta make sure I take some more Tylenol and once I get this breakfast Imma go and sit down cause I feel my chest getting tight. "Imma get yo breakfast right now John. I just gotta lil headache and you hollering ain't gonna make me go no faster!" Lord what the world? Everything just went black. Where is John? "Hattie? Hattie?" I could hear John's voice but I couldn't see him and I think I'm on the floor.

"Pastor Miller thank you for coming to the hospital. My mother talks about you all the time and I have been meaning to come to your church."

"It's Julian right? Your mother talks about you all the time. She is very proud of you. How is she doing?" "The Doctors...." Tears pour down Julian's eyes til he can't speak anymore then his brother Troy comes over to inform me of Sista Hattie's condition. "Cancer! My mother's cancer came back and she didn't even tell us! The doctor is saying that she is in her last hours Pastor. I am mad as hell! Why didn't she tell us what she was going through? Why does everything with her always have to be about the Lord? Why wouldn't she allow us to help her? If only I knew. I can't believe that my last conversation with my mother could be the damn argument we had last night. Tell me Pastor how can your God do this to her? Troy was visibly angry and of course there were no answers that I could give. "Troy, there are so many people in this waiting room praying for your mother. I am praying for your mother and we just have to believe that God's will shall be done." A young lady walked in and I could only guess

that it is Hattie's youngest child, Alana who I had
not seen in years.

"Julian, Troy where is daddy? Is he in the
room with Mama? I wanna see my mama. Where
is my mama?" Julian is the sweet one in our
family. He always knows how to say to me what
needs to be said while Troy is condemning and
condescending. "Lana we both already been back
to see mama and I think you should go now." I
could see in my brothers' eyes that he had lost
hope for our mother. The first time she was sick
we knew she would pull through because my
mother puts on the front like she's oh so sweet but
in all actuality she is stubborn as hell. The Pastor
took my hand and said she would walk back with
me. "Hi Lana, I haven't seen you since you
graduated. I saw the baby and she is a cute, little,
fat thing. I'm going to walk back to the room
with you if that's alright? My mother always
speaks highly of Pastor Miller and she just feels
like God even though I don't think I know what
God feels like but its something about how she

spoke and her presence that just made me feel
good. "Sure Pastor, I would really appreciate it if
you could." Walking around to the room to see
my mama felt like a mile. The hospital smell is
sickening and for some reason my legs feel weak.
I am beginning to understand why they have these
rails on the wall for you to hold on to. Pastor
Miller is really kind. She helped hold me up
while I walked to see mama. Then about four
steps before getting to mama's room 1302, I see
Iesha and the other nurses helping to hold my
daddy up. "Daddy! Daddy! What's wrong?" My
daddy is a skinny man but he always seemed like
a giant to me until today. When I looked at his
face he looked like a frightened child. "She gone
Lil Pea." I aint never seen my daddy cry until
today.

"Julian, are you ok? I've been calling you
and I was beginning to get worried." I knew that
the last time Julian and I got together we had a
great love making session. I bought him this
beautiful blue suede coat that he wanted so he

couldn't be mad at me. There was a long silence on the phone that was almost uncomfortable and all I could think is "Please don't let him say that he doesn't want to see me again." "Ursula my mother passed away Sunday." Oh my God how could I be so inconsiderate? "Julian I am so sorry. Where are you? Is there anything I can do or anything you need?" "Right now we are preparing for the funeral and Troy is trying real hard to use his connections so that our other sister can come to the funeral." I hate funerals but I will make sure that I am there for Julian and whatever it is that he needs. This is the time for me to prove to him that I am there for them and he should love me.

"Troy, how are things going with the arrangements?" "Thanks for calling Pastor. We have everything set. The ladies from the church have done so much for us so there really wasn't much for us to do. It really feels good to have so much support. I never knew that my mother touched so many people. It seems like every time

I turn around somebody is bringing food, cleaning the house, praying or just calling. We have so many flowers that we've asked people to donate to her favorite charity in lieu of flowers." "Your mother was loved by so many Troy. She truly was a woman of God who touched lives." "Pastor I'm kind of glad you called because I do need to ask a favor of you." "Sure Troy anything what do you need?" "Well I know that you have a large congregation and that you know a lot of people. My family never talks about it but we have a sister, Ty Quesha. Her mother and my mother used to stay in contact sometime ago and I really don't know where she is or what she is doing but I know that mama kept track of her. My mother always said that if anything happened to her she wants us to find Ty Quesha." "Ok Troy, give me all the information that you have and I will try my best to find her.

Ty Quesha

I loved Marquez. Now I am sittin in this jail waitin on dem to decide what they gonna give me. I don't really remember what happened or how I even got to dis point. What the hell! I don't even give a damn anymore whatever happens – happens. Besides, it ain't the first time I been in jail. I tell my kids I'm going on vacation and hell it really ain't that bad. When I'm in a 6x6 by myself it gives me time to think.

I read in this book one time that most little girls that grow up with teenage mothers are more likely to be teen mothers, end up in trouble or be on welfare so I guess I'm a damn statistic. I was born to a teen-age mother, seventeen to be exact. My mother was a beautiful woman in her younger years. She had beautiful full lips, satin brown skin and when she walked down the street, it was enough to make a sane man lose his mind. The shape of her body could be described as a Coca-Cola bottle, but sometimes a beauty so divine can be seen as a curse instead of a blessing. She met a

man one-day that swept her off her feet. My
mama never had nothing because her mother died
when she was fifteen and she was raised by an
alcoholic, abusive father. When my daddy took
interest in her and she saw that he had some
money, she took the chance to see what would
happen. She didn't care if he was married and I
guess neither did he. Nine months later I showed
up.

To hear people tell it. The trip to the
hospital when my mother was in labor was
anything but traditional. She had been partyin all
night and was a little *tore up* as we say. The car
was full of her partyin friends who were all a little
lit up with liquor. To hear the story, I am
surprised we even made it to the emergency room.
I was born at 6:30 am and not a moment to soon.
The liquor had not yet worn off so my moms was
feeling no pain. When I was brought home,
which was my mothers friends house, I was
placed in a drawer with a pillow put in it and that
was my crib. I guess since there was really no

planning for the pregnancy that there was no
planning for anything else. Plus money was
funny and I don't mean that in a laughing manner
either.

I basically had a normal life up until the
age of seven when an event happened that seemed
to change the rest of my life for the worse. My
mother had moved in with a man a few years after
I was born. Therefore, as I grew not knowing any
better I began to call this man daddy. He was the
only father I knew and he was good to my mother
as far as I could see. I never knew them to fuss
or fight and if they did they never did it around
me. I remember a Christmas that we had; it was
the Christmas that I realized there wasn't a Santa
Clause. I was sleeping and I heard a lot of noise
down stairs in the house that we were living in. I
slowly crept down the stairs making sure that no
one heard me and I saw my mommy and my then
daddy wrapping my gifts. I can't really remember
how I felt because a seven year old really don't
care about who gives the gifts, just as long as they

get them. I had such a good time that year, need less to say it was the last good Christmas that I would have for a long time.

My mom and that man broke up. She said, "things just weren't working out." I was so sad and really could not understand what the whole relationship thing was all about. As if the break up was not enough for me, my mother decided that she was going to give me at seven years old another devastating blow. She told me that the man that I thought was my father was not my father and that she was never going to get back with him again. We then moved back in with my mother's friend name Peaches and seemed to start the process of life all over again. My mother and I went from living in a two-story home in Atlanta to moving to a cramped two-bedroom project on the Southwest side of Detroit. My mother's friend had four kids of her own, and several rotating live in boyfriends so my mother and I had to make our way on the floor sometimes. I would have taken the bathtub but

Rayqwan had that. The twin-sized bed that reeked with pee pee was where Keisha and Toya slept. Puddin who was the youngest child, slept in the bed with Peaches when the men weren't around.

When my mother and I made a pallet in the living room, every night we would take the blankets and sheets and lay them on the floor to try to make it soft enough to lay on. I really wouldn't have cared that much if it weren't for the *rats.*

At night I would get as close as I possibly could to my mother in hopes that her body could protect me from the rats that would creep out of their holes at night. I would not only worry about the crawling rats, but I also had to worry about the ones that walked on two feet. Sometimes when mama and her friend would have their all night parties they would tell us kids to all go into the room. We could still hear the sounds of laughter and music through the door. Sometimes it would get so good to the grown ups that they would break out into a fight or make us kids get out the bed and come dance for them.

After the party was over I still had to make my pallet in the middle of the floor. Mama would be sound asleep and snoring real hard, and that's when the rats with two feet would come out. They sometimes would creep out of mama's friend's room and sometimes they would creep out of the kitchen. No matter what way they came, it would make me scared. I remember the night I saw the most horrible two-legged rat, the one I called Mr. Smelly. He appeared one night while mama was snoring. It was the first night I think I learned how to pray.

Mr. Smelly came into the living room from Peach's room but I expected it to come out of the black trash bag sitting in the middle of the kitchen floor. I heard the creek of the wooden boards of the floor and the squeaking sound of mama's friends' bedroom door as it opened up slowly. I drew closer and closer to mama's snoring body, but it was not enough to wake her as she was surrounded by empty bottles of Malt liquor and Seagrem's gin. I saw the shadow of the rat as it crept around the corner. I wanted to scream but I was too afraid. I could feel the sweat running down my forehead and down my back. That's when I saw him for the first time. I was face to face with Mr. Smelly, the most hideous of all of the rats. When I saw him he was scarier than I thought he would be. He stood about six feet tall and to me at the age of eight, he was a giant. His eyes were blood red and very wide and he had teeth like a shark.

As he drew closer, I thought that I would die from a heart attack because I could hear my heart beating in my ear. The closer he came the closer I got to my mother hoping that he would see her and leave. It seemed to me like the rat knew that my mother would not save me, but I continued to hope. The only thing that I remember is the pain and the agony of the rat clawing at me with his horrible large claws. I thought I was going to die. Every time I would open my eyes I would be face to face with this gigantic monster. The smell of it was so sickening that I wanted to throw up. The minutes seemed like hours to me with the rat grabbing and gnawing at me. I felt like I was his only meal for the day because he continuously pressed his teeth against my teeth and constantly tried to ram his tongue down my throat like he wanted the food out of my stomach. I gasped and tried to break for air but the hold that was on me was to great. Then something happened that I really could not understand, the Barbie undies that my mama and pretend daddy had bought me for the previous Christmas was being yanked off of me. But why would a rat want my undies?

I lay there on my back with tears rolling down my face while the left claw of the rat held me down and his right claw tore the rest of Barbie off of me. Then it looked at me with those huge horrible red eyes and laid itself on me as if to smother me. I felt something against the inside of my right leg moving slowly up towards my

stomach and then a sharp pain had me to scream
which triggered Mr. Smelly's claw to fly over my
mouth and my nose. "Mama please wake up,
Mama please wake up!" I kept screaming for my
mama but by this time the rat had drug me across
the room into the kitchen that was hidden by a
counter and mountains of black trash bags.
"Mama please wake up!" I hear myself
screaming but the words can't penetrate through
the claw of Mr. Smelly. I don't know what is
happening and I really began to get scared. I can't
breathe! "Please get off me", I thought and for the
first time I prayed. I tried remembering when
Mama Hattie would take me to church on Easter
and how the Pastor would say that anytime you
feel lonely or scared pray and God will hear you
and help you. So I prayed in my mind imagining
what God would look like as my 8 year old body
was torn apart by Mr. Smelly. I was trying so
hard before Mr. Smelly finally devoured me to
remember the prayer that Mama Hattie had taught
me. "Jesus Jesus Jesus!" is all that I could

remember under the last breath that I felt that I was going to take. Mr. Smelly's claw blocked air from coming in my nose and out my mouth and he weighed so much that my shaking scared body was almost coldly still. Then right when everything started to get blurry and I started falling asleep, there was a "creak" sound, the kind of sound I heard when Mr. Smelly came out. I think Mr. Smelly heard the sound to because as soon as the door "creaked" the rat leaped off of me and ran out of the front door. It was five-year old Toya finally getting up to go to the bathroom instead of peeing in the bed. She never did see me lying there crying, she just went into the bathroom did her business and came out. I couldn't breathe normal but as soon as Mr. Smelly leaped up I started to be able to see again. I slowly got up after that and I don't know how, but I went to the front door to make sure it was locked. I picked up Barbie and went to put her back on but there was blood running down my leg. I went into the bathroom and used a red wash

cloth to clean up so that Ms. Peaches wouldn't be
mad that I dirtied up her rag. I then blew my
nose, dried my eyes, and limped back over to the
pallet on the floor where mama was still snoring.
The clock said 3:45am a time I will never forget
because it was the first time I prayed and the first
time God answered my prayer. I never saw Mr.
Smelly again.

I moved to Atlanta when I was age 17.
Mama was on that crack and she was in and out of
jail until they found her body over off Caniff in
Detroit. Some Nigga she was shacking up with
strangled her to death with a belt or at least that's
what I heard. The police never found the dude
that killed her but my Nigga Poncho did and I was
more than pleased to put a bullet in the dude that
killed mama. We dumped him over in the Detroit
River where most of the dudes that owe Poncho
money were. My mama introduced me to Poncho
when I was fourteen and out of the seven children
that I have, two of them are by him. Poncho made
me his bottom bitch and treated me better than the

rest of his hoes. I ain't never worked a corner and most of the time I could pick and choose my tricks. My hustle has always been the pole and before I moved to Atlanta we were making some real good money. When the Feds started busting all Poncho's houses and seizing everything it was to hot for me to be in Detroit so Poncho sent me and most of his money down to Atlanta to work for his boy Pete. If you a stripper and you look half way good, Atlanta is the place to be. Pete looked out for me and at that time my four kids. He set us up in this nice condo near downtown and had me running half of Atlanta. In return I gave him some and ended up getting pregnant by him. After I dropped our son, I started working in Magic City and then moved on up to private shows with celebrities because that's where the real money is. I got pregnant by an NFL player when I was 20. Pete and I were raking in the change black mailing that Nigga because he's married and at the top of his career. For him to have a baby by a stripper would have destroyed him and most of his endorsements would have backed out. I was driving a Benz, living in a condo, making good money and I got to see Mama Hattie. I was living and riding high until Poncho was murdered by the police. I didn't go to the funeral because I was in the hospital birthing my son. Besides they had to have a closed casket because the news said the police shot Poncho thirty-two times. I guess he forgot to pay them.

"Would the defendant please rise?" My attorney say he gonna get me home but he ain't. I knew what I was doin. They say I'm crazy but I aint. Marquez dead ass got what he had comin. I don't give a damn if his mama did cry on the stand. If I could I would stab her 27 times in her damn back for birthing that nasty mothafucka.

"Ty Quesha, dear please stand up." Mr. Goldstein smiles at me like he just know everything's gonna be alright but it ain't. I'm facing some serious time this go round or maybe even death. Looking back in the courtroom I take one last look at all seven of my kids that the social worker had heart enough to stay with after they testified. Looking back at how all this went down I would do it all again. If they send me to death then I will just have to damn die but as long as I live no Nigga will ever touch my kids!

Justifiable homicide! "Mr. Goldstein, please explain to me what is going on. You mean I'm not going to jail?"

He stands their looking at me pitifully like the Pillsbury Dough Boy. Mr. Goldstein is old as hell and only about 5'6 in height but I guess because I'm only 5 feet tall or because his ass just got me off he stands as tall as God.

"Ty Quesha dear we are going to get you all processed out and then we will talk more. For right now you should be thinking God because you really must have some good friends in the right places because Judge Van Horn has a reputation for being harsh on ex offenders." He keeps looking at me with this baffled look as if he doesn't even know what happened. "You are going to be required to take psychological counseling and therapy but basically the Judge decided that your act was justified." Mr. Goldstein is the only white man that has ever treated me kind without wanting sex in return and he has been working this case for a minute and I have tried on several occasions to give him some. All this time I thought that Pete or T.O my NFL baby daddy was paying for him because I knew I couldn't afford him but I was soon to find out that it wasn't a nigga that was looking out for me.

"So Ty-Ty how it feel to get off like a fat rat?" I really don't feel like talkin to Keisha right now. The only reason I keep her around is because she is Pete's other baby mama and it helps when I can use her dumb ass to get him mad at her. When he is, that makes him treat me better and alienate her ass. I swear sometimes that this trick don't have the sense that God gave an ass when it comes to dudes. She actually think that Pete love her ass because he come and get the booty every now and then. I remember she told me that she couldn't understand how he could come and sleep with her and then not call her the next day. I was like "Seriously? You that damn dumb?" I thought it but didn't say a word because I wanna keep her thinking I'm on her side. "Keisha please don't ask me no questions just roll them trees up cuz my nerves is bad right now. Mr. Goldstein talkin bout I got an appointment with some attorney at 3 o'clock today". Keisha paused and looked at me with this dazed and confused look like she really wanted to ask me a question but didn't know how to ask since I just told her not to. I'm beginning to understand why Pete keeps her around. She is not the finest chic or the brightest but this heffa can find some of the best Kush around and knows how to roll it just right. Thank the Lord for Chicken Head hoes! "I see the look on your face so I'm gonna tell you right now I don't know what the hell he want or who he is. All I know is that Mr. Goldstein told me that I don't have nothing to worry about and that he

would be there for me." "Okay well its already
two o'clock and you ain't even got no clothes on
yet and you gotta get across town to see them."
Whenever she go to thinking that's when this chic
start hurting herself. "First of all Keisha, I got my
stuff together from last night so I ain't gotta worry
about it." I look over at the brand new white
leather furniture in the living room and how my
purple sundress is laid across it waiting for me to
slip my size 2 into it. I love my sundresses
because they show off my sexy ass tattoos. One
day Imma catch Mr. Goldstein old ass slippin and
then its on and poppin like pancakes.

Got my herbs in me, got my dress ironed
and on, whisper of Jadore and these cute ass
strappy platforms. I think I'm ready to walk out
the door just gotta brush some gel on my baby
hair to make it lay down just right. This the first
time I've been able to get ready this quick,
probably because the kids are still in care until I
finish this last session. I hate the fact that
Shaquan braided my hair this damn tight, now I

gotta take some Tylenol's before I go to sleep tonight. "Keisha Imma drop you off on my way."

"Good afternoon my dear won't you come in and take a seat?" The office of William Murphy and Bradley is what it said on the outside and I was talking to Mr. Murphy. I don't think I've ever seen a more bourgeois nigga in my life. He sitting up here with his fancy suit and bow tie like white people really gonna take him seriously.... Nigga please. "Ms. Jackson you were asked to be here because there is a matter of a will that we must discuss with you. Does the name Hattie Mae Johnson ring a bell for you?" At first I was sitting down but now I'm sitting at the end of my seat because if he is talking about a will and Mama Hattie in the same sentence that means that she is dead.

To Be Continued....

Thank you so much for reading the Sister Hood of Insanity Volume 1.

This novel was written for you. We are so excited and have already started working on The Sisterhood of Insanity Volume 2. We know that most novels don't usually have discussion questions in the back but that's why Urban Light is not like other novelist.

We ask that you please take this novel to your book clubs, small groups, family and friends and talk about some of the life struggles that the women of the sisterhood go through. We hope that you can identify with the characters and continue to follow their journey in the next volume.

After you have the time to read and discuss the book we would love to hear from you and get your feedback. Please email us at urbanlight@urbanlightshine.com. Thank you again and we appreciate your support God bless.

Urban Light

DISCUSSION
QUESTIONS

URSULA

1. Would you date a younger man? If not why not and if so why?

   _____

   _____

2. Why do you think Ursula is dating the younger man that she is with?

   _____

   _____

3. Is Ursula happy with her relationship?

   _____

   _____

4. Would you consider Ursula a confident woman or an insecure woman?

   _____

   _____

5. Is there anything about Ursula that
   you can identify with?

   _____

   _____

6. Have you ever changed your
   physical appearance to impress
   someone?

   _____

   _____

7. Would you consider plastic surgery?
   If so what work would you have
   done?

   _____

   _____

8. What did you think about Julian?

   _____

   _____

9. Would you date Julian?

_____

_____

10.. Where do you feel the relationship between Ursula and Julian will go?

_____

_____

LAUREN

1. How do you feel about Lauren?

   _____

   _____

2. Do you think that Lauren and Terrance will get back together?

   _____

   _____

3. Should Lauren tell Craig e about what happened with her and Al?

   _____

   _____

4. Is there any other help that Lauren should seek?

_____

_____

5. What do you think about Lauren?

_____

_____

6. What do you think about Al?

_____

_____

7. What do you think about Craig?

_____

_____

8. Do you think that this is having an
    effect on Lauren's children? If so
    why? If not why not?

_____

_____

9. Do you journal?

_____

_____

10. What do you think will happen
    next?

_____

_____

ALANA

What do you think about Alana?

_____

_____

Is there anything about Alana that you
can identify with?

_____

_____

Have you ever had an affair with a
married man?

_____

_____

If you are married have you ever had an affair? If so did you leave your marriage?

_____

_____

Is it Alana's responsibility to tell the wife about the baby?

_____

_____

Are there any legal actions that Alana should take? Why hasn't she taken them? Do you think that she will take them?

_____

_____

Where do you think the relationship
with Alana and this man will lead?

_____

_____

What do you think about the man in
this story?

_____

_____

Do you think that he really loves
Alana?

_____

_____

How does Alana feel about herself?

_____

_____

REVEREND BRENDA MILLER

Should Pastor's be appointed to
churches if they are single?

_____

_____

Could you be lead as a church
congregate by a female pastor who is
single?

_____

_____

Do you think that Rev. Brenda's
personal feelings affect her ministry?

_____

_____

Have you ever been lonely?

_____

_____

Are you single and want to be married?
If so do you know why you are still
single?

_____

_____

Is it okay to be frustrated with God?
Do you feel that God hears your
prayers?

_____

_____

What should Rev. Brenda do about how she feels?

_____

_____

What do you think about Rev. Marquis?

_____

_____

Where do you think the relationship will go with Brenda and Marquis?

_____

_____

IESHA

How do you feel about Iesha?

_____

_____

Do you think Iesha is a good mother?

_____

_____

Should single parents date?

_____

_____

Do you think that Rob would have
married Iesha ?

_____

_____

What about Iesha's health?

_____

_____

Do you think Iesha is over Rob's death?

_____

_____

Do you think Jaheim and Iesha will have a long-term relationship? If so why and if not why not?

_____

_____

What role does Reggie play in Iesha's life?

_____

_____

How do you think Iesha met Reggie?

_____

_____

What would you like to see happen to
Iesha?

_____

_____

TY QUESHA

Have you ever been or know someone
who was molested?

_____

_____

What do you think about Ty Quesha's
mother?

_____

_____

Do you think Ty Quesha is a good
mother?

_____

_____

What kind of childhood do you think
Ty Quesha had?

_____

_____

With the information that you have
what do you think happen?

_____

_____

With the information that you have
what verdict would you render?

_____

_____

How do you feel about Marquez
mother?

_____

_____

Do you think this could have been avoided?

_____

_____

What do you think will happen to Ty Quesha's children?

_____

_____

What do you think about Mr. Goldstein?

_____

_____

HATTIE

What do you think about Hattie?

_____

_____

Who is the Hattie in your life?

_____

_____

Can you relate to Hattie?

_____

_____

What do you feel about Hattie's husband?

_____

_____

Is there any hope for your marriage?

_____

_____

Do you have a Cookie?

_____

_____

What do you think about how Hattie was raised?

_____

_____

What would you like to see happen to Hattie's children?

_____

_____

Do you feel she should've divorced?

If married - how much time do you spend
at church compared to at home? Why?

GINGER SNAPS BABY

Would you consider Ginger Snaps Baby successful?

_____

_____

Do you think she is talented?

_____

_____

Did you like Ginger's poem?

_____

_____

As a woman have you ever entered into a sexual relationship with a woman?

_____

_____

If so, why do you think you had this relationship?

_____

_____

What do you think about Angel?

_____

_____

Do you feel that Zora would still be Ginger's friend if she knew her lifestyle?

_____

_____

Is Ginger a lesbian?

_____

_____

How do you feel about homosexuality and religion or those who profess Christ?

_____

_____

Do you think that Ginger will ever find a man?

_____

_____

NIKKI

How do you feel about Nikki?

_____

_____

Do you think Nikki may have a
problem with her weight?

_____

_____

Do you think Nikki still has feelings for
Derrick?

_____

_____

Do you feel that all men cheat?
Should Nikki call Derrick for closure?

_____

_____

What do you think about Troy's first impression?

_____

_____

Should Nikki call Troy again?

_____

_____

What would you tell Nikki if you were her mother?

_____

_____

Would you consider Nikki a successful woman?

Is there any thing Nikki should change about herself?

_____

_____

RENEE

How do you feel about Renee?

_____

_____

Do you think that Renee is successful?

_____

_____

How does Renee feel about her life?
Is it wrong to live for success?

_____

_____

How do you feel about powerful
women?

_____

_____

What do you think about how Renee grew up?

_____

_____

What do you think about Renee's friend?

_____

_____

Who is the Renee in your life?

_____

_____

What would you like to see happen to Renee?

_____

_____

Describe the most powerful woman in your life and why is she powerful?

_____

_____

_____

Made in the USA
Charleston, SC
26 July 2011